HIT AND RUN

A gripping crime thriller filled with twists

CATH STAINCLIFFE

Detective Janine Lewis Book 2

JOFFE BOOKS

Revised edition 2022
Joffe Books, London
www.joffebooks.com

First published by Allison & Busby Limited
in Great Britain in 2005

This paperback edition was first published
in Great Britain in 2022

Cover art by Nick Castle

ISBN: 978-1-80405-413-0

To my brothers, Paul (I got the hint — you read the book) and David.

NOTE TO THE READER

Please note this book is set in the 2000s in England, a time before smartphones, and when social attitudes were very different.

PROLOGUE

Marta was straightening Rosa's hair. Rosa watched in the mirror, occasionally pulling faces to tease her friend. She'd already helped Marta, who wanted her blonde hair crimping in tiny zigzags; now it was Rosa's turn. Marta took another length of dark wavy hair and clamped it between ceramic plates. Rosa winced; she could feel the heat on her scalp.

'Steady on,' she spoke to Marta in the mirror. They always spoke Polish when they were alone together. 'I want it straight not barbecued.'

'Stop moaning. You have to suffer for your looks.' Marta pulled the tongs the length of the hair then released it. A couple more swipes and she declared it done. Rosa smiled, admiring herself. She hoped it wouldn't rain or she'd go all frizzy again.

'Going in early?' Marta unplugged the device.

'Bit more cash.' Rosa rubbed her thumb and fingers together.

'See you later then.'

'Sure.'

* * *

When Marta left, Rosa let the façade drop. She had butterflies in her stomach already and an unpleasant tightness in her chest. As a child she'd loved to play hide and seek, the thrill of hiding and running, the exquisite shock of being found. But this was no game, she knew that. The chance that it would all work out still lingered but she knew it was a dim hope. Whatever happened she couldn't afford to be caught.

When she left the house, anyone watching would have seen a lovely young woman walking swiftly. If they had looked a little longer they would have noticed the determination in her face and the set of her shoulders, perhaps a trace of fear in her gaze.

* * *

Two girls on bikes found the body, not a dog-walker as is often the case. Barely dawn, the pair had stuck to their pact to cycle to school. Their parents had allowed them to take the scenic route along the riverside with admonitions that they must stay together, take a change of shoes, not do anything silly. After all, it was argued, that route was safer than braving the heavy rush hour traffic chugging into Manchester or out to the motorways. And youngsters needed more exercise these days.

The girls were skirting the path beneath the motorway flyover when one of them had glimpsed the log-shaped bundle stuck on the weir, buffeted by other debris that clung on the edge, water streaming around it.

She braked and stood astride her cycle, thinking for a moment it was a manikin, someone's idea of a joke to put the thing there, like those arms sticking out of letter boxes. Calling to alert her friend, she continued to stare at it; taking in the ribbons of dark hair in the water, the curve of an arm, something bright around the wrist, a plastic bottle perhaps, shreds of black plastic obscuring the rest. It was the colour of that arm, a greyish white, like mould on meat, which finally made her realise what she was looking at. That filled her throat with fear and sent shock stinging into her fingers.

CHAPTER ONE

Not late, not yet, just nearly. Janine Lewis steered seven-year-old Tom out of the house and towards the car. Day two back at work and it still felt like a Herculean labour to get the kids sorted and herself to the police station on time. It was bound to get easier, wasn't it? Please? Somebody?

At least baby Charlotte had behaved well for Connie, the nanny, yesterday — not even crying when Janine, her stomach knotted with that back-to-school feeling, had left. The older two, Eleanor and Michael, more or less got themselves ready and out. Eleanor, still neat in her new High School uniform, desperately careful to have all the correct books for each day. Still getting used to the transition. And Michael off to sixth-form college, enjoying the freedom of wearing his own clothes, a flexible timetable and — if the amount of grooming he was doing was any indication — the attention of girls. Michael had reacted badly to his parents' separation but he seemed to be over the worst now; he'd settled down to his coursework, stopped seeing the other lads who'd been such a bad influence.

Connie came out on the doorstep holding Charlotte. The nanny wore her long hair in a single plait which helped emphasise her Hong Kong origins.

Janine walked back and kissed her baby, nuzzled the fine hair on her head. Charlotte made a little sound, an appreciative murmur.

'Bye-bye, my best girl,' Janine told her. Turning to Connie she added, 'Ring me if there are any problems. I should be back by six unless anything new comes in.'

Her first day back had been deskbound: forms and reports to absorb, catching up on the new initiatives that the police force had introduced since she'd gone on maternity leave, updating her ID pass and parking arrangements and reviewing security procedures in the building. She'd needed that space; her head still felt fuzzy from lack of sleep, her mind cluttered with all the tasks associated with being a mother of four, one of whom was still an infant.

Now, climbing into the car, she looked forward to the delicious luxury of being able to make coffee in her office and drink it while still hot, the novelty of not being interrupted by a cry. Compared to the demands of being at home, work felt like a doddle. After six months up to her ears in nappies she had probably developed cabin fever.

Lunchbox! She clambered out again, grabbed Tom's lunchbox from the top of the car and put it on the passenger seat. Tom was strapped in, listening to his personal stereo, his head nodding to the music. She gave him the thumbs up, got in and started the car. When she pulled out into the main road the traffic was busy and slow.

She had dreaded and anticipated her return to work in equal measure. Being part-time would have been the ideal but it simply wasn't an option if she wanted to progress in the force. And she did. She relished the challenges of leading major enquiries, of working with a team. That was the real heart of the job: the detecting, the hard task of uncovering the real story, getting to the truth behind the tragedy and ultimately finding justice for the dead and their loved ones.

It was a bright day, cool but not cold enough to be frosty, with a fresh breeze. The trees had shed almost all their leaves now; an odd one clung on here and there, flapping against the blue sky. A flock of pigeons wheeled overhead as Janine made slow progress through Didsbury village. The street was lined with shops, restaurants and estate agents, the road edged with parked cars. The property market was still booming and every spare speck of land was being developed into luxury apartments for young professionals.

Janine's mobile rang and she pressed the hands-free answer button.

'Janine?'

'Richard?'

Her colleague, Detective Inspector Mayne to give him his full title. She gleaned a sense of urgency in his tone. She glanced in the rear-view mirror checking that Tom was still tuned in to his music, anxious he shouldn't overhear anything that might be inappropriate.

'Suspicious death,' he said bluntly. 'Body in the Mersey, Northenden. They're pulling her out now.'

Janine swallowed, braced herself as she felt the spike of adrenalin kick in. 'I'm on my way,' she told him.

Outside the school, Tom pulled away from her to dash through the gates. Janine called him back, holding up his lunchbox. He turned and ran, his arms outstretched, plane-fashion. Grabbing the box, he wheeled away but not before Janine had a chance to plant a kiss on his head.

Janine returned to her car and was just drawing away from the kerb when she saw a blue Mercedes coming, far too fast, down the centre of the road. Near the gaggle of late arrivals waiting to cross, the car braked fiercely with a squealing sound. Janine saw the child flung to one side, the small body flying limp like a puppet, then landing hard. The car shrieked to a halt a few yards ahead. Janine grabbed her phone, her heart thumping hard in her chest. A knot of people gathered round the injured girl. With a sickening feeling, Janine recognised her as a classmate of Tom's — Ann-Marie Chinley.

Her mother was screaming, kneeling beside the unresponsive child. 'Ann-Marie! Ann-Marie! Oh, my God, somebody help me!'

A powerful sense of shock was palpable in the atmosphere; Janine could almost taste it, acidic like metal, harsh and electric, galvanising them all.

Janine pressed 999, speaking as soon as the operator answered. 'Ambulance. Little girl's been knocked down. Outside Oak Lane Primary, Didsbury.'

One of the women wore a nurse's uniform, most likely working at one of the nearby hospitals, St Mary's or Manchester Royal Infirmary; she began checking the girl. 'It's all right, love. Try and make you comfy, eh? Can you hear me, Ann-Marie?'

Janine heard an engine rev, watched stunned as the Mercedes set off again at speed. She pulled out after it, sounding her horn and mounting the pavement to pass the onlookers.

Her mind had the bright clarity that comes with stress; she concentrated on the number plate, V384 ZNB, memorising it before the car turned out of her view. Using the police radio she got through immediately: 'Attention all units, Detective Chief Inspector Lewis reporting RTA Oak Lane Primary, Didsbury. Driver failed to stop. Pedestrian injured. Blue Mercedes, registration Victor 384, Zulu, November, Bravo. Heading west on School Lane.'

She spotted the Mercedes again, turning right into Wilmslow Road. She activated the emergency sirens and flashers on her own vehicle and increased her speed. The traffic was still heavy; cars and vans and several buses chugging towards the city centre. They responded to the siren, pulling in so she could overtake. At the next junction she followed the Mercedes as it took a sharp right turn and roared away. She kept up with it along Fog Lane, fighting to keep control on the bends and where the road narrowed. The suburban street was a blur of privet hedges, red brick walls and stone gateposts that fronted the family houses. Despite her best efforts she couldn't get a clear view of the car's occupants; the windows were tinted glass.

Traffic lights ahead remained on green as the Mercedes took another right. Round in circles, she thought. She increased her speed again and edged closer. 'Vehicle now on Parrswood Road heading south from Fog Lane.' They rode through the Parrswood council estate with its distinctive cream rendered houses, built in rows of four.

In dismay she watched as the car approached the School Lane lights. It didn't slow even though they were on red. Janine kept close. The Mercedes crossed the junction directly into the path of an oncoming van. The getaway car swerved violently and Janine, on its tail, screamed and rammed her foot on the brake, feeling the slam of the seatbelt as the car bucked and stopped inches from the shocked van driver. The Mercedes disappeared over the hill ahead. Frustrated, Janine hit the steering wheel. Damn, damn, damn.

Her radio crackled with news. 'Victor 384, Zulu, November, Bravo. Mercedes reported stolen 22.00, Monday, 17 November.' Stolen the previous evening. She groaned. The culprits would be even harder to find.

Returning to the school, she found the ambulance just leaving; the little girl was alive but unconscious. She rang Richard and filled him in. The group of witnesses remained; one woman was crying, wiping at her eyes repeatedly, automatically rocking the tall coach-built pram she'd been pushing. Others were talking about the accident, their voices hushed but edging now and again into hysteria. When traffic officers arrived shortly afterwards Janine spoke to the man in charge, giving a résumé of what had happened. Finally she got back in her car and set off for Northenden, feeling shaky and hollow and cold.

* * *

The car park at the side of the weir, next to the camping suppliers, was already awash with police vehicles. As Janine parked she saw the first news crew arrive, piling out of their van with cameras, flight cases and cables.

A scenic spot. It would make for good visuals — unlike the rows of terraced houses, dull semi-detached frontages or bleak alleyways that were usually the staple setting for local murder stories.

The river, olive brown and swiftly flowing, curved between steep grassy banks. The sweep of the motorway flyover above cast part of it in shadow, making the water there almost black. On the far bank were concrete buttresses that were part of the water management for the area. The land was low here and the Mersey often flooded, submerging the nearby golf course and playing fields along the valley.

The stretch of water behind the weir was pitted with eddies and ripples and patterned with fractured blue reflections from the sky above. Below the weir, the river seethed, a gushing torrent of white and silver, before regaining its equilibrium.

Fifty yards away, towards the large riverside pub and parallel with the weir, Janine could see the white incident tent that was shielding the corpse. Scene of crime officers, clad in white, were going about their business. She dressed in her own protective suit and locked the car.

At the edge of the car park, she gave her name to the officer keeping a log of entry to the site. She could see Richard near the tent, dark-haired and a head taller than many of the others. Slim in his long, black, winter coat. Attractive looking, if you liked that type, and she did. She'd almost slept with Richard years ago, but her engagement to Pete held her back. There was still a pull between them, apparent in the flirting and teasing they enjoyed. But now, in the aftermath of Pete's departure and Charlotte's arrival, she knew she wasn't ready for a relationship with anyone. Not yet. Never mind the risks of getting emotionally entangled with someone at work.

He nodded as she reached him, his head tilted in concern. 'You OK?'

She sighed. 'No, not really.' She paused, took a breath. 'She's only seven, the little girl.'

'How is she?'

She looked away across the water. It was easier than meeting his gaze. Stopped her from getting tearful. 'They've taken her to hospital. She's in Tom's class,' she added.

'Close to home.'

Janine bobbed her head, sniffed hard, swallowed. 'So,' she gestured towards the tent, 'what's the story?'

'Female. The Rivers Authority guy reckons the body will have gone in upstream. Flows east to west.'

Which way was east? Janine tried to get her bearings, pointed in one direction, thinking if that way was south . . .

Richard set her straight. 'That's east — Stockport.'

The river marked the boundary between the city of Manchester and the adjoining town. 'We got a time frame?'

'Not yet. But she's reasonably intact. Day or two.'

The pair of them covered the few yards to the plastic tent. As she stepped inside Janine caught the rank smell of river water and the sweet reek of death. She opened her mouth; breathing that way would cut out the stench that made her gag. She focused on the body. The face was shrouded by long, wet, dark hair, tangled with bits of straw, flotsam from the river. Tattered bin liners covered the torso. Janine glimpsed raw flesh on the face, in between the banks of hair, and on one exposed thigh. She noticed straps at the ankles and colourful plastic dumb bells.

The pathologist, Dr Riley — Susan as Janine knew her — was still bent over the body. She looked at Janine.

'Looks like she was strangled; bruising to the neck. The face is very badly damaged.'

'From the water?'

'I don't think so.'

Janine grimaced. The woman's face had been spoilt deliberately.

'ID?' Richard asked.

'Nothing. No clothing. There's a wound to the upper right thigh. The surface skin removed.'

Janine looked back at the body. 'A tattoo?'

'Could be.'

'Or a birth mark?' Richard suggested.

The pathologist nodded. 'She was weighed down. Gym weight strapped to each foot, one round the neck.'

'But she didn't stay down?' Janine said.

'Not heavy enough. And as the body filled with gas . . .'

They needed to identify the woman as soon as possible. Knowing who she was would be the key to the direction the investigation would take. 'If we move fast,' Janine said, 'we can get an appeal on the news this afternoon.' She looked at Susan. 'Can you give us vital statistics?'

'Twenties, dark hair. Five foot six, slight build.' Richard entered the details in his daybook.

'Perfect.' Janine told her. 'How soon can you do the post-mortem?'

The pathologist smiled. 'You queue jumping?'

'Moi?'

'See what I can do.'

'And the report?'

Susan raised her eyebrows, folded her arms.

'One's no good without the other,' Janine studied her.

'Early afternoon — if I skip lunch,' she said dryly.

'Very overrated, lunch,' Janine countered as she made to leave the tent.

CHAPTER TWO

Butchers and Shap, sergeants both: the one big-boned, plump and ginger-haired, the other trim, sharp-faced and balding, caught the call when the Mercedes was found. On their way back from a training day on community liaison that had been cancelled due to illness, it was Butchers whose ears pricked up as the radio squawked into life. 'Stolen vehicle, wanted in connection with RTA, driver failed to stop. Blue Mercedes, registration Victor 384, Zulu, November, Bravo. Reported on waste ground off Dunham Lane. Unit to attend.'

Butchers jerked his head at Shap.

'Base, we've got this,' Shap said.

Butchers took the next left, his homely face set rigid with determination.

When they reached the windswept location the car was still ablaze; thick, oily smoke coiled up into the air carrying the stink of burning rubber and plastic. Hard to tell it had been a Mercedes, let alone a blue one.

Butchers sighed volubly.

'Flambé.' Shap said. 'Owner's going to be made up, isn't he?'

'Better get forensics on this.'

Shap gave a derisory snort. 'They'll be lucky. Be like getting prints off a cinder.' Nevertheless he dialled the number, reported what they'd found and took details of the registered keeper — a Mr James Harper — who had reported the theft the previous evening.

'You up for this?' Shap nodded at the wreck.

'Why shouldn't I be?' Butchers glared at him.

'Well, just . . . you know . . .' Butchers had only confided in Shap about it all once: a very drunken night before either had got their stripes when all the other coppers had gone home and just the two of them were left, slurring words and spilling drinks. Butchers had turned out to be a sentimental drunk though he hadn't wallowed in his own story, just mentioned it when they were talking about why they'd joined the force. Shap had asked a few questions and Butchers had given him the facts, though not much more, and then the talk had turned to something else, something less personal and that had been it. Not a whisper since.

Now Butchers just kept staring ahead.

'Fine,' Shap raised his hands in surrender. 'Forget it!' That's the way you want to play it, he thought, then fine, no problemo. Maybe back then Butchers had been so pissed that he hadn't remembered telling Shap at all? Shap had no idea if anyone else at the station knew. Probably not. Well, at the end of the day it was Butchers' funeral; Shap had given him a get out clause and he'd turned it down. What else could he do?

James Harper had what the estate agents would call a desirable residence on the outskirts of Sale, south of the city. Butchers ran an eye over the façade with approval. Some of these more modern houses were slipshod but he knew quality when he saw it; even the wood cladding was patently high-grade material and the dimensions were generous. Integral garage, picture windows above. Nice landscaping in the front, low maintenance gravel and alpines. Solid hardwood door, though the rest was uPVC. Must be making a bob or two, Butchers thought, place like this and running a Merc. All right for some.

'Detective Sergeant Shap, Sergeant Butchers,' Shap made the introductions. 'You reported your car stolen last night?'

Harper's face lit up with surprise. The smile accentuated his prominent cheekbones and the deep dimple in his chin. 'You've found it? I thought it'd be halfway to Russia, by now.'

Butchers grimaced.

'If we can come in, sir,' Shap said.

They followed Harper through to his lounge. Harper smoothed his hair back over his head. Long at the back. Compensation, Shap recognised immediately, the deep forehead testimony to a receding hairline. Shap had never gone that route. Kept his short.

'We have found the car,' said Shap, 'but it's a write-off.'

'A write-off?' Harper's face fell. 'I've only had it three months,' he said, exasperated.

Butchers took over. 'I'm afraid your vehicle was involved in a road traffic accident earlier this morning. Hit and run.'

Harper's expression changed to one of shock. 'What happened?'

'Little girl knocked down. She's in hospital.'

'That's terrible.'

'We're still trying to find the driver,' Shap explained. 'Did you see anything when your car was stolen?'

'Not a thing. I was in the house when it happened, as well. Car on the drive, crook-lock, immobiliser, the works. I couldn't believe it . . .'

Butchers and Shap exchanged a look. Harper wasn't going to be much use to them. Just another statistic in the auto-theft figures.

* * *

'It was definitely our side of the boundary, not Stockport's?' Detective Chief Superintendent Leonard Hackett glared at Janine and Richard.

'Yes, sir,' Richard replied.

'Shame. So, Janine — you'll take the rudder?'

He wanted her to lead the enquiry. She glanced at Richard; while she had been on leave, he had acted as lead officer and she knew he hoped to keep that level of responsibility.

Richard cleared his throat. 'But, sir, I thought I'd be . . .'

Hackett frowned. 'DCI Lewis is back now.'

Janine stepped in. 'Sir, I'd really like to pursue the hit and run.'

'Well, Mayne can lead on that.' He gave a bright, vacant grin.

'Can I suggest we team up and cover both?' Janine said, trying to find a way she could stay involved with the accident.

Hackett pursed his lips, pulling the face that had led Janine to nickname him The Lemon. 'The troops need to know who's in charge. Clear chain of command.' He thought for a moment. 'No. You should lead on both, Janine.'

She felt Richard stiffen.

'Obviously the murder is the priority,' Hackett added.

'Yes, sir.'

She could see the tension around Richard's mouth, the irritation in his eyes, though he didn't say anything.

Hackett nodded in dismissal and the pair of them stood and left his office.

Once they were out of earshot, Richard let rip. 'He was happy enough while you were on maternity leave. I cleared three major enquiries for him, three!'

'It's not you — it's him,' she told him. 'You'll get there. He can't put it off forever he'll have to promote you. He did the same with me.'

Richard sighed, slapped at the wall in frustration.

'You'll get it, you will.'

She recalled her own promotion to Chief Inspector. Not the most favourite day of her life. Oh, the promotion had been a triumph — it was what followed that had floored her. Going home to celebrate with her husband Pete, only to find him in bed — yes, their bed — with the home help. End of celebration, end of marriage. She'd given Pete a second chance, felt obliged to, seeing as she was six months pregnant with baby number four, but Pete had picked Tina the cleaner instead. Work had kept Janine sane then. A place apart from all the miserable pain of splitting up.

Richard sighed harshly again, shook his head, still annoyed.

Janine looked at him. 'So, you going to stay here and have a paddy or shall we get on with it?'

He glowered at her for a moment, and then relented, knowing she was right. He jerked his head in assent.

'I'm off to the post-mortem,' she told him. 'Pull everyone in for two. Incident room one.'

* * *

When his mobile rang, Chris Chinley was flushing out a central heating radiator in the backyard of the house where he was working. The black sludge guttered out from one end as he poured water in the other. Not been cleared for maybe forty years, full of silt and grit.

He grunted at the ring tone and lowered the radiator, balancing it against the weathered brick wall. Only a small yard in spite of the size of the house: three storeys, four bedrooms, high ceilings, each with the original plaster rose and covings.

Chris pulled his phone from the back pocket of his jeans, already anticipating another customer. Business was booming. A shortage of plumbers had coincided with soaring demand. People wanted two or even three bathrooms in a property, ensuite to the master bedroom, showers and bidets, sometimes a jacuzzi. He'd actually done a hot tub the previous month, in Hale, Cheshire — richest area outside of London.

He didn't recognise the caller number on display. 'Chinley's,' he said.

Chris listened to the voice on the phone. He swallowed hard, ran his free hand over the coarse, close-cropped hair on his skull. Shaking his head, he stared down at the flagstones, watched the pitch-black water stutter from the radiator, thin to a trickle, then snake along the cracks between the flags and into the gutter that ran out to the alley at the back.

* * *

Post-mortems were never pleasant but Janine attended them whenever she could. It helped her maintain a good working relationship with the pathologists but, more importantly, it was something she felt she owed the victim. To bear witness. The aroma of the river still clung in the air. The woman lay, still wrapped in the rubbish bags, on the dissecting table. Her face was a horrible mess; Janine took it in with a glance and cast her gaze elsewhere.

She listened intently while Susan worked on the woman's body, sharing in the meticulous process of description and observation as first the external, then internal examinations were made. Susan photographed the body, took measurements and made notes of its appearance before cutting away the wrappings and removing the plastic gym weights. After taking more photographs and x-rays, including dental x-rays, she took samples from the wounds on the face and thigh, scrapings from under the nails and a number of hairs. Then she began the process of dissection: opening the body and examining, removing and weighing the major organs. Susan took blood samples from the heart, tissue and fluid from the lungs and a sample of stomach contents for toxicology. She swabbed the orifices.

The smell affected Janine more than the sight of these things. The unmistakeable offal odour of liver and lungs. And the sound of the saw, when Susan opened the skull.

Janine thanked her when the procedure was over and offered to get her a snack from the canteen.

'Something to keep me going?' Susan said wryly.

Janine smiled, acknowledging the tactic. She wanted the report in time for her briefing.

'Chicken korma on granary, black coffee, banana.' Susan removed her gloves with a flourish.

Janine bowed. It was the least she could do.

* * *

By two o'clock the photographs of the body and the riverside site were already up on the boards in the incident room. A video loop was running on a monitor, detailing the recovery of the corpse and location shots of the immediate vicinity. Maps on one wall depicted the river and push-pins in blue indicated locations that would be searched to try and determine where the body had entered the water. Three of these pins had already been replaced with yellow ones — these places had already been visited and nothing had been found.

The incident room was on the fifth floor of the building, windows on three sides giving a clear vista out across the city centre and nearby Salford; rooftops, canals, the quays and the wide Manchester sky; here and there the distinctive outline of a landmark building: the prow of the Lowry, the triangular peak of Urbis and a sea of cranes bobbing and wheeling in the never-ending business of construction.

Janine moved in front of the boards, signalling to those milling about that they were ready to begin. Over twenty people occupied the room, most in civilian clothes, one or two uniforms. The hubbub of chatter died down as people slid into seats and opened their notebooks. Keeping detailed records at every stage of an enquiry was a detective's lot: nothing was said, acted upon or looked into without an entry into an officer's daybook. It became second nature, ingrained.

Janine smiled in welcome. 'I'm DCI Lewis; some of you have worked with me before.'

'Thought you looked familiar,' Butchers said, 'something's different though.' He mimed a bump on his stomach.

'Still got yours, haven't yer?' Shap shot back at him, nodding in the direction of Butchers' paunch. Butchers glowered, sat up straighter.

Janine continued, introducing the senior officers to the room. 'Detective Inspector Richard Mayne, Sergeant Butchers and Sergeant Shap. Any uncertainties about procedure, any questions or problems,' she told the DCs, 'these guys,' she gestured to the two sergeants, 'are your first port of call. This will be our dedicated incident room. So what have we got?' She turned to the boards. 'Unknown victim was seen in the river at Northenden just before eight this morning. First priority is to try and identify her. Our second to establish where she was killed.'

'It's likely that the body entered the river to the east,' Richard said, pointing to the wall map and indicating the large area they were searching, 'so that narrows it down,' he added dryly. 'We're searching all known access points within a five mile area.'

Janine raised the report she held. 'The post-mortem confirms the victim was in her early twenties. Malnourished as a child and since. Pregnant, about two months.' She noted the rustle of unease at that bit of information. 'Signs of recent sexual activity. Cause of death — strangulation. Time of death estimated to be within twenty-four hours of her discovery The trauma to the face occurred post-mortem, as did the removal of skin from the thigh. And I don't think he was collecting souvenirs.'

'Someone wants her incognito,' said Shap.

'Heavy; rectangular object used on the face, possibly a brick,' Richard elaborated. 'The lab will do a drugs and toxins screening.'

'They've also recovered some tissue from under her fingernails; we're running DNA on that. Anything else?' She invited contributions from the floor.

'We've sent details through the system, missing from home — no match as yet,' Butchers supplied.

Shap raised his chin. 'Have we got anything from the post-mortem that gives us the scene?'

'No,' Janine answered. 'A day in the river hasn't helped. They'll be examining remnants of bin bags used to wrap the body and the gym weights.'

'Could be a fitness fanatic — the weights?' Butchers suggested.

'Bog standard,' Richard shook his head.

'I reckon everyone's got a set like that,' said Janine, 'shoved in the cupboard along with the foot spa and the yoghurt maker.' People smiled. 'The pathologist also noted some blue staining on the left ankle, knee and hip.'

'More tattoos?' Shap asked.

'No. Here.' Richard pointed to the photographs, tracing the discolouration around the hip and knee. 'It's faint, no particular shape.'

'They'll come back to us when they've more on that,' said Janine. She raised her head and looked round the room at the team before her. Some of the young officers were setting out on their first major investigation; some would never have seen a dead body before. They had no idea how much the case would dominate their lives in the weeks to come or of the peculiar mix of tedium and excitement that would characterise the work they had to do: the referencing and cross-checking, door knocking and listening, the endless paperwork. And, here and there, the surge of action, the buzz of closing in on their quarry; the breaks that made it all worthwhile.

'We're looking for a lot of help from the public on this one; it'll be all over the papers, but you lot, discretion. Please — don't natter about it down the pub — or at the gym.' Janine paused. When she spoke again her voice was reflective, a shade quieter, forcing them to listen harder, focus on what she was saying. 'You all have something to bring to solving this case. If you have ideas — share them. If there's some detail that sticks out — check it. Don't be afraid to ask if anything confuses you. We're here to learn — all of us. The day you stop learning is the day you stop being a good detective. Sergeant Shap will allocate teams for the initial stages and briefings will be held daily, first thing until further notice.' She gestured at the boards again. 'A young woman, killed then mutilated. Who was she? Who wanted her dead?

That's why we're here.' She motioned to the picture from the riverside, the one of the body on the grassy bank: sodden hair, a slim wrist, the graceful hand, fingers gently curved. 'That's who we're here for.'

CHAPTER THREE

Chris Chinley's heart cracked when he saw Debbie. She was curled into a chair in the waiting area, her head down. No one else about. 'Debs?'

She started, stood up and his arms went round her. She was tiny; her head barely reached his chest. When he first met her, he thought of her like a bird: all fine bones and a fast heartbeat and eyes bright and alert. But the impression of physical frailty concealed a surprising strength. When things had been really bad with the baby, the one they lost, it was Debbie who had held it together, who'd clung on and kept on and dragged him with her.

'What's happening?' he asked. 'Where is she?'

'They're trying to stabilise her, she's still in Casualty.'

'Can we see her?'

Debbie shook her head. Chris stepped back a pace; he needed to sit down. She sat beside him; her fingers sought out the end of the zip on her top and she plucked at it.

'Debs?' He needed to know: how is she, will she be all right? But was too scared to ask. Christ, he hated hospitals. With the baby, Debbie's first pregnancy, they'd been in and out. Bed rest and observations, scans and tests and, at the end of the day, none of it had worked. Nearly three years to conceive and the baby miscarried at five months. Then Ann-Marie, their little miracle.

'Debs?' He begged her again.

She began to tell him about the accident, speaking quietly in fits and starts, trying to steady her voice. She was a nurse; she would know the score. He feared she was building up to bad news, thinking that if she started with the where and the when, the facts of the matter, told it all in sequence, that he'd somehow be able to take the truth when she got there.

'We were waiting to cross. I was talking to one of the other mums. Ann-Marie,' her voice lilted dangerously, 'was waiting. There was nothing coming . . . I know that . . . I remember that, and she stepped out. I remember thinking, it's OK, there's no traffic . . . Then this car, it just came from nowhere, so fast. All at once, they were there . . . Ann-Marie,' her voice broke and she made a flapping motion with one hand, the other darting up to press against her mouth. 'They drove off,' she blurted out.

He put his arm around her and pulled her close, his chin on her head. He felt hot inside, his heart swollen with rage. They hadn't stopped! The image of Ann-Marie tossed, falling, scalded him and his eyes and throat ached. He ground his teeth together.

'They were very quick,' Debbie spoke eventually. 'The ambulance. Really quick. She was unconscious.'

He couldn't speak but he nodded. She didn't add anything else. More pictures danced in his head: his daughter crushed and bloodied, limbs bent this way, that way, the wrong way. Eyes closed, peaceful. Eyes open flaring in pain. Her body twitching.

Some minutes later, Debbie sat up, pulled away from him and wiped at her face.

He stared at the wall opposite. Another row of polypropylene bucket chairs, a notice board with signs on reminding people of the hospital's no smoking policy, of the cost of missed appointments, exhorting people to ring up if they couldn't attend. He gazed at the fluorescent lights, at the vinyl flooring and the skirting board and the chairs opposite.

'I should have held her hand,' Debbie cried. 'I always hold her hand to cross. I always make sure she holds my hand.'

'Shhh, Debs, don't.' He put his hand on her leg and pressed. 'Don't.'

She stood impatiently, wrapped her arms across her stomach, took a few steps this way and that, then sat back down. He saw her fingers start to fret on the zip again.

He closed his eyes and prayed.

* * *

Marta had woken in the night, unsure what had disturbed her. The room was dark, impossible to see anything. In the summer months the light shone through the thin curtains, making it hard to sleep late. She couldn't hear Rosa. She switched on the small bedside lamp. The other bed was empty. Her watch read three-thirty. Rosa should be back by now. The club closed at two. Was she downstairs? Marta listened. It was quiet, so quiet. A lone car in the distance but nothing else.

At home, the nights had carried different sounds. Her father's coughing had punctuated the house, night and day. And beyond that there was the noise from the steelworks, the droning of machinery, the screech and clang of metal, the shriek of hooters signalling the change of shifts and the rumble of heavy plant machinery. Round the clock, continuous production until the place was closed in the mid-nineties. Her father was thrown out of work like so many others. Her mother the only one with a wage. Her father would sit about the house or escape to the café and spend the day there with the other men, their arms pockmarked with silvery scars, the burns left by flying scraps of molten metal. When he coughed Marta imagined his lungs full of wire wool, threads twisting with each breath.

One night, after they'd silenced the machines, she had heard the howl of a wolf, her blood thrilling at the sound and a prickle of fear at the nape of her neck. She'd never seen a wolf, though her babka, her grandmother, swore they were still there if you looked carefully. Not so many, of course. A lot of the forest had gone now; they'd cut back the tall, dark green conifers, and the wolves and the bears had retreated to the wild places in the mountains.

Marta remembered a trip to the forest for her name day when she was small. She had woken to presents and flowers and cards and her father had borrowed the car from the schoolteacher. The three of them, plus Babka, had travelled for an hour and a half to one of the big lakes. A rare adventure for, apart from that day, Marta couldn't remember any other such family outings. Sometimes she wondered if it had been a dream. Babka had brought food: soft pierogis filled with lamb and blintz dusted with sugar. When she bit into the blintz and the jam oozed out the wasps had come whining around. Her parents had lit cigarettes and blown smoke at the pests.

They had been able to swim in the lake, the ones closer to home weren't safe. 'Chemical soup,' her father always said. 'Strip you to the bone and melt your eyes.' But here the water was clear and silky, achingly cold. As she struggled in, her feet slipping on the muddy stones, Marta felt the cold stun her feet and her calves. She stumbled and fell in, losing her breath at the shock of the icy wave on her back. The lake was filled by the melted ice from the mountains.

The chill water had set her father coughing and she'd had a sudden flight of fear. What if he collapsed? How would they get home? But he smiled at her, through the spasms, nodding his creased red face in reassurance.

Marta's mother was careful not to get her hair wet, sticking her neck up like a swan and moving her arms gently without breaking the surface. She was the picture of elegance, scolding Marta if she came too close with her whooping and flailing about.

Afterwards, her fingers blue and her teeth chattering, Marta sat wrapped in a scratchy towel eating the last blintz while the adults argued about the government.

Later, she went for a walk with her father, along the lakeside. The air was rich with the sharp scent of pine, the trunks of the trees dotted with the honey-brown clusters of resin. She rolled a piece between her fingers, sticky and crunchy like melting sugar, and sniffed at it.

There was one point where the undergrowth was thicker and a couple of boulders offered a stopping place. Her father paused, leaning his hand on one of the rocks. He tested the air. 'Smell that.'

Marta breathed in. A foul smell, like fly-blown meat. She felt her gorge rise.

'Bear.'

Her eyes had widened and her nerves started. What if the bear heard her father coughing? She didn't want to get eaten by a bear. Not on her name day of all things. Her father obviously agreed and they had made their way back to the women and told them there was a bear about.

Marta shivered in the chilly Manchester night. She listened again. No sound from the other rooms, or downstairs. Everyone asleep. What could she do? Nothing. Maybe Rosa had worked longer, got held up? She tried to settle herself with the explanation but knew it to be feeble. She turned the light off, closed her eyes and pulled the cover up over her head. Resorting to prayer, she rattled off a decade of the Holy Rosary, not because she particularly believed any longer but because the rhythm of the words brought some comfort, distracting her a little from her worries about Rosa.

* * *

Janine rang Connie en route to the press conference, while refreshing her make-up in the women's toilets. She examined her reflection: not bad given her broken nights. Concealer disguised any shadows beneath her large blue eyes.

'Connie, it's Janine. There was an accident outside school this morning,' she told the nanny, 'a little girl got knocked down. Tom might be upset when you pick him up.'

'Did he see it happen?'

'No, thank goodness. But some of them did, it'll be all round school.'

Janine put her make-up away and slung the bag over her shoulder.

'How's the little girl?'

'Don't know; she's in intensive care.' She used her free hand to open the door. Richard was still waiting for her in the corridor with an official release from the press office. She took it from him, began scanning it as they walked briskly towards the conference room. 'And I'll be working late, so–'

'You know I'm going out?' Connie interrupted.

'Yes. I've asked Pete to come over for six-thirty.' Pete was her main fallback now. Her stalwart neighbour and good friend Sarah had moved away for a better teaching job and her parents were getting past the point where she felt able to rope them in as babysitters. Pete worked as an air traffic controller at Manchester Airport. His availability depended on his shift pattern but it only took him twenty minutes to get to Janine's from work.

'How's Charlotte?' Janine asked Connie.

'Fine. Sleeping a lot.'

'Not at night, she isn't,' Janine muttered.

* * *

Journalists with notebooks, cameras, microphones were gathered waiting for them. Richard and Janine took seats behind a table at the front of the room. Janine read from the prepared statement, ignoring the flashes from the welter of technology pointed at her.

'This morning the body of a young woman was recovered from the River Mersey. We're treating the case as murder. She is a white woman, believed to be in her twenties, five foot six inches tall, with a slim build and long dark hair. We think she also has an identifying mark on her right thigh. We would like to appeal to the public to help us find out who she is. If you know of anyone answering that description who has gone missing, then please ring in straight away and let us know.'

She paused and then invited questions.

'How was she killed?' A young reporter with severe black clothing and hair to match.

'How long has she been dead?'

'Was she drowned?'

Others joined in and Janine raised her hands. She would take them one at a time but there was little she could add to the information she'd already given them. The questions and her 'no comment' or 'we can't say at this point in time' were part of the familiar jousting between the force and the media. Keeping relations sweet was essential: inappropriate or inaccurate coverage could seriously hamper their efforts while responsible reporting could generate help and vital information from the general public. All a matter of balance. And Janine reckoned she was good at balance, juggling home and work, seeing all sides of a story keeping the plates spinning. Must be circus blood in my veins, she thought wryly as she nodded to the journalists.

* * *

The rest of the afternoon flew by in a whirl of activity, mainly setting up systems to support the enquiry and ensuring everyone knew how to process data so it would be most useful. Information from the teams out in the field would pass to officers here. Everything would be entered in the computers and the most salient facts written up on the boards in the incident room.

At four-thirty Richard took a call from the forensic science lab. 'She hadn't been drinking and no evidence of recreational drugs,' he told Janine.

'What did we have on stomach contents?'

'Just partially digested coffee and biscuits.'

'So she'd not been wining, or dining, or clubbing it.'

Richard began to add the notes to the boards. 'Domestic then?' He paused and looked at her, marker in his hand.

'It's unusual,' Janine shook her head, 'most domestics, they panic. If they do cover their tracks it's token. This — the weights, the river, the face — it's very extreme. I know we can't rule anything out but I reckon there could well be more to it.'

Richard cocked his head inviting her to elaborate.

She shrugged her shoulder. 'I don't know. We'll just have to find out, won't we?'

CHAPTER FOUR

Marta knew as soon as the policewoman on the television news began speaking. She felt the skin on her face contract, her ribs tighten, her tongue thicken in her mouth. A falling sensation, as though the ground had staggered beneath her. She was alone in the sitting room, the other girls busy working. They had been jittery all day, ever since Marta told them Rosa hadn't come back. No one had said very much, just asked the same questions as Marta had: where can she be, is she all right, what has she done?

Marta tried to trick herself again, to pretend it was all a silly mix-up, ludicrous to think it could be Rosa. Then the policewoman said about the mark on her leg and she knew it was true.

Oh, Rosa. She swallowed, gagged a little. Went through to the kitchen to get a drink. The water was clean here, tasting sweet and peaty. Not like home. Home. I was like a rabbit in a cage, Rosa had told her. A two-bedroom house in the suburbs outside Krakow had housed Rosa, her mother, her elder brother, his wife and child and her younger brother. Rosa slept in the living room. I couldn't breathe, she had said. No space to turn round, no privacy. Like Marta, she had tried to get work but there were so few jobs, and the ones she could go after were poorly paid, the conditions miserable. Packing, cleaning, waitressing. Rosa had dreamed of another life. A job that paid for some nice clothes, a bedroom, independence. It wouldn't happen in Poland but in Italy, the UK, Germany . . .

Marta steadied herself against the sink, looked out across the red brick walls of the backyard, the roofs opposite with their TV aerials and chimneys. Pigeons clustered on one.

As Marta had before her, Rosa had asked around — did anyone know of work in the UK? Scraping together enough to pay her passage, she had arrived nine months after Marta; came in the same way. A lorry from Krakow market to Prague. At a place near there, a service station, they had transferred to a minibus. Ten of them in all, in Marta's group. Giggling and excited but falling quiet whenever they saw a police car or approached a border. Coming in from Poland they didn't need visas. Once they were through customs the driver, a sullen man called Josef, took their passports back. The boss would keep these until their resettlement fee had been paid. He had arranged jobs and accommodation for the girls.

Marta had known dancing was a euphemism from the start. But what did it matter? If you switched off while you were working, avoided trouble with the clients, it was only a job. Inside too, not like picking fruit for ten hours a day like some did, stooped over in all weathers or working in an unheated shed packing meat or stinking fish. Marta sent a little money home knowing it made a real difference and she saved a little. One day she would move on. This was just the bottom rung but it didn't mean she'd be stuck here for the rest of her life.

The police didn't know the woman from the river was Rosa — would they find out? What if they came here? What if they found Marta and the others? The thought brought a swirl of nausea with it, a sour wash at the back of her throat. She raised the tumbler and drank again, her fingers pressed tight and pale around the glass.

* * *

At six o'clock Janine turned off her laptop, packed her bag and turned off the lights in her office. She found Richard in the incident room. Several DCs were still staffing the phones and taking calls a result of the appeal for information. A cleaner was emptying bins and clearing away paper cups and food wrappers from some of the desks.

Janine shrugged into her coat. 'Right, I'm calling home and then I'll be at the hospital.'

It was dark now and from the office they could see the city lights: the red neon letters spelling out CIS at the top of that tower, the stacks of office blocks with row after row of rectangles aglow, below and in between glimpses of streets smothered in the haze of orange street lights and strung with the endless pulse of white headlights and red tail lights.

'You've not heard anything?' he asked her.

Janine shook her head. 'Don't know whether that's good or bad.' She'd rung an hour ago and been told there was no change.

Shap came over, his eyes bright, eyebrows raised. 'Think we've got something on the murder, boss. Several calls coming in about a woman, Rosa, worked at the Topcat Club. Never showed up last night.'

'You'll take a look?' she said to the two of them.

Richard nodded.

'Place in town, back of Victoria Station, belongs to a Mr Sulikov,' Shap said. 'Couple of the callers wouldn't leave their names but we've one from another dancer there.'

'Dancer?' Janine queried.

'It's a lap dancing club.' She could see Shap fight to keep the grin from his face. 'Someone's got to do it, I suppose.'

* * *

Janine was halfway down the corridor that housed the intensive care wards when she spotted Debbie and Chris Chinley in the parents' lounge.

Debbie was small, petite, fine-boned. She had large brown eyes and black, curly hair, Ann-Marie her spitting image. By contrast Chris was a stocky man, big-boned with huge hands, a thick neck and something of a boxer in the square shape of his face. He nearly always had stubble around his chin — the sort of man who had to shave twice a day. Both worked tirelessly for the PTA at school. And Debbie was one of the parents who volunteered to help read with the children who needed extra support.

Now they sat side by side. Chris had a bleak, blank look on his face while Debbie's was hidden in her hands, though Janine could see her shoulders jerking. Janine's stomach clenched. Bad news.

Janine knocked lightly on the door and went in. Chris gazed at her, shook his head. The man looked absolutely desolate.

'I'm so sorry.' Janine went to sit beside Debbie who looked up, her face smeared with tears and make-up, her nose swollen, lips cracked.

'I'm so . . . so sorry.' Janine repeated.

Debbie, tearing a soggy tissue in her fingers, turned to her. 'They said they did everything they could but it wasn't enough. It wasn't enough.' Her voice rose and faltered. Janine put her arms round her. Could there be anything worse, she thought? She blinked hard and listened to the woman weep.

* * *

Richard was driving as they made their way along Cross Street in the centre of Manchester, past the rebuilt Marks and Spencer store at the bottom of the Arndale centre, past the giant windmills and water feature of the Millennium gardens and the Triangle shopping centre and the Printworks leisure complex opposite, both plastered with giant screens relaying adverts and entertainment.

Richard took a small side street, then another in the area behind Victoria Train Station and parked in front of the Topcat Club.

'You been here before?' he asked Shap as they approached the entrance.

Shap frowned. 'Not sure.'

Richard looked at him.

'Well,' Shap defended himself, 'they all look the same after a few bevvies.'

There were photographs of the girls in the entranceway, scantily clad but nothing that you wouldn't find in the tabloids.

Richard and Shap made their way up to the bar — more photos of girls lined the bar area. There was a sprinkling of customers and two girls pole dancing in a central area. Tables and chairs were laid out informally and around the perimeter were some seating booths affording a little more privacy. Shap surveyed the place in appreciation. Richard gestured to the barmaid.

'What can I get you?' she asked.

'Mr Sulikov here?'

'No.'

'This is his place.'

'Yeah. But he's not here. You want the manager?'

Richard nodded.

A couple of minutes later she returned with the manager. The bloke did a double take when he saw Shap.

'You know each other?' Richard asked.

'Detective Inspector Mayne,' Shap said introducing them. 'James Harper, owner of the stolen vehicle involved in this morning's accident.'

Richard's nostrils widened and he raised his eyebrows, staring hard at Mr Harper. 'Small world,' he said, his voice sharp with suspicion. Janine would want to hear about this.

* * *

Feeling wretched, Janine was halfway home from the hospital when her mobile rang summoning her to the nightclub. It took her ten minutes to reach the city centre location. It was dark already, a single star, Venus if she remembered rightly, the only thing bright enough to cut through the light pollution that hung over the city. Janine looked at the pink neon Topcat sign flashing on and off and braced herself.

The music was loud and the decor shiny. Glittery pink stripes ran through the wallpaper, glossy brown fake leather covered the booths and seats. The platforms where the girls danced were lit from above and below by pink spotlights. The girls looked very young and wholesome in spite of all the flesh on display. There wasn't much of an erotic charge to the dancing as far as she could see; repetitious and detached, curiously passionless.

She could see Richard and Shap at tall stools near the bar. Apparently enjoying the floor show. Neither of them saw her approaching.

'Interview concluded already, then?'

Richard jumped at her voice. 'Thought we'd wait for you, boss.' He smiled sheepishly and slid off the stool. 'This way.'

She followed him along a corridor; plush red carpet and silver flock wallpaper. 'We've got a name.' Richard told her. 'Rosa Milicz, Polish.'

They reached a small office, the door ajar. Richard stepped inside and she followed. 'Mr Harper,' he introduced the man seated at the cluttered desk. 'DCI Lewis — she's heading the enquiry'

Harper was about Janine's age, late thirties, maybe early forties if he'd weathered well, tousled light brown hair, longish at the back, clean-shaven. He had an aquiline nose, high sculptured cheekbones, a cleft in his chin. He stood and shook her hand; he was slightly stooped and his suit was rumpled. He wore a collarless shirt beneath it. Janine noticed photos on the wall, names beside them: Suzy, Fleur, Carmen.

'Rosa.' Harper passed Janine a head and shoulders photo. Janine studied it. She looked young, younger than Janine had imagined, vivacious. Someone had strangled her, Janine thought, squeezed the life from her then ruined that lovely face.

'She didn't turn up for work yesterday. The description — it could be her. I missed the news but Andrea, one of our dancers, she rang in.'

'Was Rosa married?' Janine asked him.

'No. Over here on her own.'

She turned to Richard. 'Put in a request to Poland for dental records asap.'

He nodded.

'Can we see her employment file?' Janine asked.

Harper coloured slightly, rubbed at the bridge on his nose. 'Ah, well, the girls are freelancers, you see. They sort out their own tax and national insurance. Of course we pay public liability for the premises.'

'Wages?' Richard said.

'Cheque or cash. I think . . .' He stood and crossed to a filing cabinet, rummaged through and pulled out a file, riffled through it. 'Yes, Rosa was paid in cash.'

'Rosa's address?' Richard said.

'No, we don't seem . . . no, sorry.'

'That usual?' Janine regarded him carefully. She noticed one of his eyes was more open than the other, one eyelid drooping, though she couldn't read the expression in them. 'Employing someone and not even having their address?'

Harper looked a little uneasy but said nothing.

'Surely you'd have taken her details when you hired her?'

'The girls get a form to fill in — all those details — we just don't seem to have one for Rosa. I've no idea what's happened to it.' He slid the drawer shut.

'You don't own the business?' Janine clarified.

'No, I'm just the manager. The owner's abroad.'

'That's Mr Sulikov?' Richard said. 'His first name?'

'Konrad.'

'What can you tell us about Rosa?' Janine asked him.

'Nice girl. Reliable, turned up for her shifts on time. Never any problem. That's why it's so hard to understand.'

'How do you mean?' Janine asked.

'Some of them — they get in a mess: drink, drugs, boyfriends. Or they're breaking the rules, putting themselves at risk. Topcat's for dancing.'

'Strictly ballroom,' Richard said.

'We keep it clean. No touching, no tango. Some girls push it, or they make private arrangements with the punter outside these walls. We can't protect them then.'

'Anything make you think a punter's involved?' Richard asked him.

'I don't know what to think. All I'm saying is Rosa did her job, no fuss, no bother.'

'Did you know she was pregnant?' Janine wondered if Rosa had known herself. It had been early days. And if she had known had it been welcome news or not?

'No,' Harper looked surprised, 'she never said anything.'

Janine didn't like her cases colliding like this. It sparked her sense of mistrust. 'Your car was stolen last night?' She let the words hang in the air.

'That's right.'

'It was involved in a hit and run accident this morning. The little girl's died.' She felt Richard's eyes on her. 'Now Rosa.'

Harper looked puzzled. Janine waited it out, watching him. Wondering if he would volunteer any more information, try and explain the sequence of events, the glaring coincidence. Harper said nothing.

'Mr Harper,' she said, 'I'm going to have a look around, talk to people. Please give DI Mayne all the details you have about Rosa. Last time you saw her, the names of any regulars she danced for, friends she had.' Janine paused in the doorway. 'Death seems to be following you around. I'd try to think of anything that might help us.' No harm in shaking his cage a little, letting him know that she didn't buy the little-white-hen-who-never-laid-an-egg routine.

CHAPTER FIVE

Andrea, the girl who had rung in, agreed to talk to Janine but in spite of her cooperation there was a distrustful edge to her manner. A lot of people acted like that with the police. Sometimes they had reason to.

Andrea had creamy brown skin, short curly hair. Young again, and wary. She toyed with the ashtray, played with cigarettes and the bangles on her wrist, avoiding eye contact for much of their conversation.

'Did Rosa have any distinguishing features?' Janine began.

'A tattoo, on her leg, a rose. Her right leg — that's why I rang. It all seemed to fit. Is it her?' She glanced at Janine.

'We think so.'

Andrea compressed her lips, looked back at the table. 'Who do you think did it?' she said fiercely. 'Who'd do a thing like that? Why?'

Janine shook her head.

Andrea tilted her head back, blinked hard at the spotlights on the ceiling.

'What was she like?' Janine asked.

'Pretty quiet, really. Not shy, didn't let people push her around or anything. Just never said much about herself.'

'Any problems with the clients? Or anyone else?'

Andrea shook her head.

'You were both here Sunday?'

'Yes.'

'Finish at the same time?'

She nodded. She rooted in her handbag, pulled out a packet of baby wipes and Janine glimpsed the snapshot of a toddler. Andrea found the cigarettes she was looking for. She slid one from the packet.

'Who left first?'

'I did.'

'And you didn't see her again? Was there a boyfriend?'

Andrea shook her head, lit her cigarette.

'Do you know where she lived?'

'No.'

Was the denial a little too fast? Janine looked steadily at the girl.

'Look, we worked together, that's all.' Andrea said defensively. 'She was a nice kid but I don't socialise with people from here. None of us do. It's just a job. She had a room somewhere, that's all I remember her saying.'

'Is there anything else you can think of that might help us?'

'No.' She took a drag on her cigarette.

Was the girl keeping something back? Or were her guarded replies her natural reaction to police questioning? 'We might need to talk to you again.'

Andrea nodded, blew out smoke and rose. Janine watched her walk across the club to leave her cigarettes at the bar. Moving away, already back on the job, smiling at clients, laughing at a remark one of them made, taking her place on a low podium.

Janine wondered what Andrea thought about working here. Did she regard it as good money, a better living than working in a call centre or waitressing somewhere? How did she feel about the customers who came to ogle her? Was one of the customers, perhaps one of the men here tonight,

Rosa's killer? Wouldn't he stay well away though? Unless he was a regular, whose absence might be remarked upon?

She could see Shap chatting to a group of men at the bar. A raucous burst of laughter. All lads together. Shap was obviously on good form. But she knew that alongside the bonhomie and the wit the detective sergeant would be mopping up every last morsel of intelligence. On the case in his own inimitable style.

* * *

Chris hadn't trusted himself to go into Ann-Marie's bedroom. Fearful that he would do something obscene: trash the place, tear down the drawings and her City scarf, the mobiles and the posters. But now he took a breath and pushed the door open. Why was it shut anyway? She never shut her door; she liked to be able to see the landing light, to be able to hear them moving about the house and call out to them. The door swung open and he took in a scattering of felt pens and bits of plastic, some cards and puddles of clothes. He'd expected it to look neater, more organised. He thought Debbie would have already tidied up. Creating a shrine.

Chris had built the beds, rigged up a slide from the top bunk and a ladder at the other end. He'd made the cupboards in the alcove, too, with drawers beneath for her clothes. The drawers had come from a big reclamation place in Hyde. Lovely wood, beech. He'd cleaned them up, sanding them and using linseed oil for a soft warm finish. He'd fixed on new handles, rejecting all the fancy shapes for some simple round wooden ones not too big for her hands and no sharp edges. After all that Ann-Marie had plastered the unit with stickers from cereal packets and the dentist. He'd felt a lurch of dismay when he'd first seen them but quickly reasoned that it didn't matter. It was her space. Just a week ago her curtain pole had come adrift and he'd been up there fixing it while she chattered to him about dogs and how their sense of vision worked compared to humans and cows and flies.

Can't fix this, he thought, and sat down heavily on the lower bunk, his head bowed in the narrow space, his hands large and useless, an encumbrance now. He stared mutinously at her old teddy, remembered making it dance as he held Ann-Marie in the crook of his arm, her sturdy legs kicking in delight. How she'd dragged the bear about as a toddler; already she was the image of her mother: the same dimples, the same wild hair.

Debbie, falling for Debbie had been brilliant. He met her through the job. She and another nurse had a flat-share in Withington, before the old hospital closed. Chris had woken her up. She'd been on nights. She was skinny and funny and pretty, even with her hair sticking out every which way. She'd made coffee and watched him work, asked him questions. She was easy to talk to.

'Reckon you need a new T-connector,' he told her, wiping his hands on a rag.

'Do I now? What's that then?'

'It's a fitting, joins all three pipes together.'

'Right.' There was a hint of a smile playing round her lips, impudence dancing in her eyes. 'You'd better sort me out then.' Her voice sounded softer and her face fell serious as she stared at him.

He had felt himself harden and a flush of heat spread along his thighs and the back of his neck.

'Pleasure.' Tension sucked the oxygen from the air. Her eyes moving up to his then back to his lips. Her hand tucking stray hair behind one ear. Her skin was pale. There was a blue vein visible in her neck. He wanted to touch it, lick it.

'I'm off Saturday,' she said.

'Maybe a drink?' His throat was dry.

'Yeah.' She smiled. The dimples in her cheeks.

They'd been married the following spring. Being with her had put a sheen on everything, a hot ball of joy inside him. Not that he'd been unhappy before that, but being with her made everything more real. Even the bad time, when they lost the baby . . . His thoughts scattered . . . Lost two babies now.

Ann-Marie, having Ann-Marie had knocked him sideways. He'd looked forward to being a dad, prayed that Debbie would go full-term. He had imagined a son, playing footie, wrestling, building castles with moats at the seaside. But nothing had prepared him for the passion he felt. She was his little shadow, following him about. She only cried when she hurt herself and soon recovered. She was fearless too, climbing chairs and desks, up the stairs in a trice. When she was four, he took her to her first City match; they were still at the Maine Road ground then; she'd sat on his shoulders and yelled along with the best of them. Debbie had left them to it, she hated football.

The thought came unbidden: if you'd just held her hand. Guilt lanced through him, swivelled in his guts. You said as much yourself, Debbie, he thought. He stared at the drawings on the wall. Ann-Marie scrawled on each one. Look, she'd said, I signed my name — scribbly like yours, Dad.

* * *

Driving home, Janine was preoccupied with thoughts of Rosa. Last seen on Sunday night. Had she died that night, after leaving the club? What had happened? An assignation turned sour or a row with a lover they'd yet to find out about? She wondered about Rosa's family, were there brothers and sisters, parents and grandparents back in Poland expecting to hear from her? She imagined the shock that would hit them when they learnt that Rosa was dead, her life ended swiftly, brutally, her body mutilated and abandoned; when the truth sank in — that there would never be another postcard or phone call. They'd never hear her voice again or open the door to greet her or kiss her. Perhaps Rosa was an orphan? With no one to mourn for her, no one to claim her remains and arrange her funeral.

Janine paused at the traffic lights in Fallowfield. Student territory here — the halls of residence that lined one side of the road were home to some of the thousands of students who came to study in the city. She watched pedestrians cross the road: an old man with a dog, both white-haired and skinny; a trio of girls, Rosa's age; a man on his own, baseball cap and jacket, a bounce in his gait. Where was Rosa's killer? Could he sleep? Could he eat and swallow and carry on with his daily life? Did he dream about what he had done? Was someone harbouring him — uneasy at his mood, at his reaction to the news coverage or his sudden interest in doing the laundry?

She was late getting back — again. She'd already rung Pete to warn him but as usual her estimate was far too optimistic. 'Sorry, sorry.' She found him in the lounge with Charlotte who was dozing in her carrycot. 'It always takes longer than I think. Kids all right?'

Pete nodded. 'Fine.'

Janine looked at Charlotte; the sleeping infant made suckling motions with her mouth, gave a little sigh. Janine drank the moment in. Then she sat down heavily beside Pete. 'God, what a day!'

'It's hard to believe.' Pete said. 'Ann-Marie . . .'

'She didn't make it,' Janine said quietly.

Pete exhaled, sat back bracing his hands against the front of his thighs.

Thoughts of the Chinleys swamped Janine's mind. 'Has Tom said anything?'

Pete shook his head. 'You going to tell him?'

'In the morning. They'll probably send a letter round from school . . .' She faltered. 'How the hell you explain . . .'

'I don't think I remember her.'

'Skinny,' Janine told him, 'curly, black hair. Her mum always did a stall at the summer fair. They had a dog. Probably still got the dog.' The ridiculous statement moved her to tears. She closed her eyes, covered her face, felt his arms go round her.

'Oh, Pete . . . could have been us . . . Tom.' She rested there for a moment then pulled away, wiping at her face. 'I'm OK.' She couldn't afford to indulge her grief — not with

Pete, anyway. 'This week — it's going to be all hours. And Connie — she deserves her evenings off.' She didn't want to jeopardise things with Connie. She'd struck lucky there. Most people said finding a nanny was a complete nightmare. When Janine had first met her she'd been impressed by the young woman's enthusiasm. 'Manchester is just fantastic,' she'd said. 'Lots going on: the Bridgewater Hall, the theatre. Do you go much?'

Janine shook her head. Connie had gone on to talk about her intention to take an evening course in business management. She had nannied while in Hong Kong but had always wanted to live in the UK. 'It's my favourite place,' she declared. Janine liked her energy. With three kids and a baby, stamina was important. She just hoped Connie wouldn't sail through her business course too quickly; she could just see her setting up her own nannying agency and making a go of it.

'I can't expect her to manage a baby all day long and then be on tap for babysitting.' Janine told Pete.

'Well, I'm on days,' he offered, rising to get his coat.

'And what about Tina?' It still stung her to say the name though she hid it well.

'Tina knows the score,' he told her.

She was relieved. She knew just how crazy her hours might get and it would be impossible without Pete to call on. No need to show too much gratitude though. After all he was their father; his spending time here was good for them all.

As Janine headed upstairs, Eleanor pounced. 'Mum, there's a girl been knocked down at Tom's school.'

'I know,' Janine said.

'What happened?' Eleanor's eyes were bright with interest. 'Did you see it, it was this morning?'

'Yes. A car went straight over the crossing, and then they drove off.'

'That's awful. Is she going to be all right?'

'No,' Janine said quietly. She saw Eleanor's face fall, her mouth part then close again. A tiny frown. 'What?'

'She died this afternoon.'

'That's awful,' Eleanor repeated, a sudden glint of tears in her eyes. Any hint of morbid curiosity vanished.

Janine hugged her. 'I don't want you to say anything to Tom, OK?'

'You've got to tell him; she was in his class.'

'I know — but don't say anything till I've had chance.'

'Why didn't they stop?' Eleanor stepped back, an edge of outrage in her expression.

'They didn't want to take responsibility for what they'd done.'

'Will you catch them?'

'We're trying. It was a stolen car so it's a bit more complicated.'

'That is so mean,' Eleanor said, shaking her head, her face miserable. Janine nodded. You couldn't protect children from the grim realities. Maybe they heard more than their fair share because of her job though she made it a habit not to bring home stories from work — or only the funny ones. But even if she hadn't been in the job, the daily news was still saturated with examples of cruelty, inhumanity, death and strife. Most of the time people compartmentalised the two worlds: the safe, private, domestic one and the big bad place out there, where awful things happened to other people. But with something like Ann-Marie's death the two spheres collided, the divisions dissolved. The wolf wasn't at the door, he was in the house.

* * *

On cue Charlotte kicked off just as Janine sank into sleep, the baby's cries jerking her awake. She felt the familiar lurching feeling: a combination of resentment at being woken and fear that her child was in distress. Picking her from the cot, she tried settling her with words, rubbing her back and feeling the tiny wings of shoulder blades beneath the babygro, circling the soft, downy head with her palm.

She tried her with a bottle but the baby didn't seem interested, there was no sign that her nappy needed changing and Janine hadn't the energy to go through the ritual of trying to resettle her in her cot. Without Pete there was always plenty of room in her bed. Opinion-makers couldn't agree as to whether sleeping with a baby was a good thing or not: a rod for your own back, dangerous even, or a natural state of affairs. Janine knew she probably got more sleep sharing her bed than if she spent time getting up and down to Charlotte who regularly woke three times a night. On that particular night, in the light of the tragedy she had witnessed, it seemed a precious thing to be able to take the child into her bed and fall asleep aware of the small presence nestling beside her.

CHAPTER SIX

First thing the next morning Janine went through to Tom's room. Plastic dinosaurs, action-men figures and small soldiers littered the carpet. He slept on his bunk. His cheeks looked flushed; his arms were flung up behind his head.

'Tom,' she said gently.

He opened his eyes. Gave her a sunny grin. He scrambled out of his duvet and down the ladder, clutching a beanie-baby dragon.

Janine sat on the sofa-bed beneath his bunk and patted her knee. 'Come here a minute.'

'Why?'

'I want to talk to you.'

He gave a small sigh and wriggled onto her lap.

'You heard about Ann-Marie's accident?'

He nodded, bounced the dragon on her leg and then his own.

'Well, Ann-Marie was very badly hurt.'

'Where?' Tom was always literal, and curious.

'Everywhere,' Janine said. 'And the doctors tried to make her better but she was too poorly.' Janine paused a moment, trying to assess how direct to be. Tom put both his hands on the dragon and held it close.

'It's very sad,' she went on, 'you see Ann-Marie died. Everybody is going to be feeling very sad about it.'

Tom was very still. She gave him time but he said nothing. She put her arms round him pulling him back for a cuddle. 'OK?' she asked.

He murmured, stood up and stretched the dragon's wings wide. 'Mum?'

'Yes,' she steeled herself for difficult questions.

'You know when I'm eight; for my party, can we go to Laser Quest?'

She bit down on the laughter rising in her throat. Bless him. 'Yes,' she said tightly, ''course you can.'

He nodded and shot out of the room holding the dragon aloft.

Once she was dressed, Janine took Charlotte down and suspended her in the baby bouncer from the kitchen doorway. That gave Janine a chance to get on with the kids' breakfasts. 'Put those two slices in when you've got yours,' she said to Michael who was hovering by the toaster. Eleanor and Tom were just finishing off their cereal and arguing about the puzzle on the back of the packet.

Charlotte pushed with her legs and whooped as the action sent her careering up and down and to and fro. 'Lovely girl,' Janine called to her.

'Hello, everybody.' Connie carefully held the elastic ropes of Charlotte's bouncer to one side as she squeezed past.

'Good show last night?' Janine asked her.

'Brilliant,' Connie beamed. 'I love the Royal Exchange.'

'Ann-Marie Chinley got run over,' Tom said to Connie. 'And Mum's going to under arrest them.'

Janine smiled.

'Arrest,' Eleanor corrected him. 'Not under arrest.'

'You are under arrest,' Tom told his spoon. 'You will, won't you, Mum?'

'Going to try.'

'She didn't make it,' Janine said sotto-voce to the nanny. 'Oh, no,' Connie said softly. Janine nodded. Charlotte squealed and swung wildly up and down. 'I best make tracks,' Janine said. 'Their toast's on.' She left to a chorus of goodbye her thoughts already turning to the list of actions she needed to get underway when she briefed her teams.

* * *

'Harper's account checks out.' Richard stepped into the canteen queue behind Janine. 'Reported the car theft at ten. Cab from home to the Casino Royale in town, meal in the restaurant there.'

Janine took the plate from the woman dishing up the hot breakfasts. His account might check out but that didn't signal the end of her interest in the man. Not by a long chalk. She pulled a face.

'I was thinking,' Richard said, taking his own plate, 'Rosa: the lack of records, no known place of residence — either someone's covering something up or she was here illegally?'

'Wouldn't be the first time.' Janine slid her tray along, stopping by the tea machine.

He continued. 'She walks in off the street, gets the job, all that cash in hand, nod and a wink stuff.'

Janine picked up the thread. 'And Harper's passing the buck, blaming Sulikov. Who's also Polish.' She glanced at him. 'Any connection to Rosa? You talked to this Sulikov yet?'

'He lives over there.'

She paid for her food and picked up her tray while Richard hunted through his pockets for cash.

'Maybe you'll get a trip to Warsaw out of it,' she said.

'Why couldn't it be Hawaii, or the Maldives?'

The pair of them sat down at a table where Shap had already finished eating.

'Meanwhile,' Janine said, 'you'll just have to grit your teeth and put up with life at a lap dancing club.'

'Shap's like a pig in muck.' Richard said. Shap snorted, rolled his eyes.

'You looked pretty comfortable yourself from where I was standing,' she said, scooping up a forkful of bacon and egg.

'Trick of the light.'

Janine took a mouthful. 'I missed this.'

Shap grinned as though the sentiment included his presence, the camaraderie or something.

'The fry up, you plonker,' Janine told him.

'How's the nipper?' Shap asked.

'She's great. Happy, insomniac.'

'Got a nanny?'

'Live in. Well — live in, go out a lot.'

'Raver, is she?' Shap's eyes lit up.

'No. Self-improvement. Night classes, theatre, opera.' Janine cut up her bacon.

Butchers came over, his face intent. 'We've got a witness on the hit and run. She saw two men get out and torch the car. Good descriptions. Height, age, clothing. One of them had red hair. We're getting a few sightings of the car coming in, an' all.'

'Good.' Janine nodded, chewing. 'Draw up a timeline. They got it when, ten?'

Shap nodded.

'Running it all night. Maybe they stopped somewhere — petrol, take-away, boozer? Got out the car and someone saw them. We'll try and keep it live, see if we can shake out some more witnesses, CCTV. Need to cross-check those descriptions with records.' She speared sausage and tomato and dipped it in her egg yolk.

'TWOCers,' Shap said, the acronym for taking without owner's consent.

'Language,' Butchers joked.

No one responded. They all knew there was no point in encouraging him.

* * *

Red hair helped a lot. Sorting through the criminal records and accompanying mug shots, as soon as the daily briefing was over, Butchers came up with a handful of candidates. Each would be honoured by a police visit. The boss came in and he brought her up to date.

'Several possible matches . . . Saul Hetherington, Clive Swan . . . and . . . Lee Stone.' Butchers was interested in Stone; he lived nearest to the area where the car had been abandoned and in Butchers' experience criminals were only too happy to foul their own nests — most not having the nous or the gumption to stray far from home to do their dirty work. If it was Stone he'd nail him; the thought increased his pulse, he'd bloody nail him. And if it wasn't Stone he'd keep on looking because this was one case he'd never give up on. 'Taking without owner's consent, carjacking, actual bodily harm, sexual assault. Eighteen months inside, released in June.'

'And the car thefts?' the boss asked.

Shap peered over Butchers' shoulder. 'Can't keep his hands off them. And last time he was going after Beemers. Stuff worth nicking. Known associate, Jeremy Gleason.'

Butchers pulled up Gleason's record. Small-time stuff, couldn't compete with Stone. Same address. The two were obviously bosom buddies.

The boss was nodding; she looked keen. 'Visiting time?' Butchers offered.

* * *

The maisonettes weren't the worst Butchers had seen but they were probably skimming the building regs when they were put up. The cheap materials and no-frills design showed in the dimensions; he bet the walls were paper thin, the residents could probably hear the neighbours fart. They'd be damp too, likely as not, the flat roofs almost impossible to seal from the endless Manchester rain.

Butchers liked his DIY, knew about making something sound, something to be proud of. Even the old council houses, the first ones, had been put up with proper brick; not breeze-blocks and plaster board and a lick of paint like this lot were.

The place was depressing: cracked glass in some doors, boarded-up windows here and there, frantic with graffiti and a shower of litter all about the place: carrier bags and take-away food trays, soft-drink cans and crisp packets wherever he looked. The bright winter sunlight glanced off fragments of glass that were sprinkled along the pathways. Time was people would have swept up, thought Butchers, but no one bothered anymore.

Shap knocked loudly on the door. Butchers rocked lightly on his heels, waiting for an answer, his throat suddenly dry. *Come on, come on.*

Lee Stone answered the door, almost seemed to be expecting them. Cocksure in his manner, he stood aside when Butchers asked if they could come in. Stone's sidekick Gleason was nervier; a tall, thin man with a shaven head, his face paled as they walked into the sitting room. The under-floor heating made the place stifling, especially with the glare of the sun coming in. There was the sweet smell of mould and fried food in the air. Butchers spotted a telltale patch of mottled plaster in one corner of the ceiling.

Butchers listened as Shap explained the background to their visit. 'We're particularly interested in the hours between 10 p.m. on Monday night and 10 a.m. on Tuesday morning,' said Shap.

Stone was sitting back on the couch, legs spread wide. His bristly red hair was cut short, he had a bullet-shaped head, thick neck and ginger eyelashes. His eyes were an insipid blue. 'Monday. Watched the box, went to bed.'

'And yesterday?' Shap said.

'Got up late.'

'After ten?'

'More like two.'

'Long sleep.'

'Clear conscience.' The man was practically sneering. Butchers felt like decking him. He turned to Gleason; he was a long drink of water, not an ounce of fat on him. 'And you, Mr Gleason?'

Gleason nodded. 'Yeah.'

'Yeah, what?'

Gleason glanced at him, eyelids flickering. 'I was here, we were both here.'

'Thing is, someone saw you Tuesday morning. Not long after nine. On the waste ground off Dunham Lane,' Butchers told him.

'Can't have.' Stone was dismissive.

'So, you don't know anything about the theft of a Mercedes or the accident which led to the death of a young girl yesterday?' Butchers couldn't disguise his irritation.

'Oh, yeah. Saw it on the news.' Stone looked from Butchers to Shap. 'Tragic,' he said, his voice laden with sarcasm. 'Well tragic.' He gave a slow smile. 'Hanging's too good for 'em.'

Four and a half miles away, at the police station, Janine was finishing a call ordering flowers for the Chinleys. As she replaced the receiver, the phone rang afresh.

'Janine? Richard. Lee Stone. Guess what he works as?'

'Interior designer? Hypnotherapist?'

'Bouncer,' he told her. 'At the Topcat Club. Harper reckons he's good on the door.'

She felt her scalp tighten and a tickling in her wrists. 'Is he now?' She ended the call and got straight onto Butchers. 'You seen Mr Stone?'

'Just left him, boss. Him and Gleason covering for each other. Stone's an arrogant prat.'

Janine told him about the connection between Stone and the club. 'I want you to get back there, bring them in. Time we had a proper chat.'

'Pleasure,' she could hear a note of gloating in Butchers' voice. 'Just made my morning, boss.'

CHAPTER SEVEN

Marta had barely slept, a dull ache in the centre of her, a sick fear about Rosa. It could happen to her . . . She imagined Rosa's family receiving the news. Terrible news from the UK. Rosa's family had been farmers for generations, working the same acreage on the central plains. Raising pigs, growing cabbages and potatoes. If things had been tough under communism they had been even worse in the wrench of change to a free market economy.

'We tried to sell some land,' Rosa had told Marta. 'But no one was interested. My father thought he had a jewel, a crock of gold but it was like trying to sell shit to a bishop. The prices fell so low that it wasn't worth driving the pigs to market. They cost more to feed than he could sell them for. Yet people were still hungry. 'People have to eat,' he used to yell. I almost felt sorry for him.' Rosa hated her father; she often called him the swine, the pig. He'd been a rough bully who had played the tyrant in his home and had few friends even among the other farmers.

Rosa's mother had moved to get work in Krakow, stacking shelves in a small supermarket. The journey took an hour each way. 'We all moved there and my father stayed at the farm. It was better for us. He went a bit mental — no one to make him feel big.'

Then Rosa's father had died. It had been three days before he was found and by then the last few pigs were going mad with hunger. There was no phone at the farm. No way to keep in touch. The authorities had been promising a connection for years. 'Not that the old bastard would have bothered,' Rosa told Marta.

The family had argued about the land. Sell it for a song or keep it. Neither of her brothers would consider taking it on and Rosa wasn't interested. Up to her neck in pig shit and cabbage stalks? No, thanks. In the end, a compromise had been reached. A cousin would lease it for five years, for a pittance, stop the place going back to the wild.

In the months after her arrival, Rosa had become depressed. She couldn't stomach the work. There was nothing to do but wait it out. Marta had tried to jolly her along, talking about what they would do when they had saved enough money. Marta would open a little shop, maybe a beauty salon. She'd always liked cutting hair and had a knack for it. Maybe Rosa would be discovered and become a model? Or do her teaching? Rosa nodded her head. She could teach English conversation to Polish kids — or Polish to people planning to travel there. Who'd want to learn Polish, Marta thought, aid workers? But she said nothing because Rosa was looking a little brighter and she didn't want to spoil it.

At Easter, Rosa seemed much better. She was dancing at the club by then and that made all the difference. She was allowed to get the shopping too. That weekend she had brought a packet of cheap felt-tip pens and fresh eggs back from the mini-market. She hard-boiled them and handed them round when the others appeared for breakfast. The girls teased her, groaning at the sentimentality, joshing her for being old-fashioned. Petra drew a face on her egg rather than a pattern but they soon fell into reminiscing and the talk turned to food. Here all they ever ate — oven chips, pizzas, ready meals — was plastic food: ready in ten minutes and hungry again ten minutes later. But at home . . .

Soon they were inventing favourite menus, boasting about the sweetest cakes, the spiciest sausage, the most perfect pierogi. 'Thick and glossy,' Marta had said, 'meat soft as butter and every vegetable you can imagine.'

How often did we actually eat like that, Marta thought; how often did we go hungry or put up with cabbage and potato day after day? Their daydreams were a far reach from the reality of life back home. But dreams didn't cost anything.

After they had eaten the eggs, Rosa had pulled a bag from the drawer where she had hidden it; spilled the bars onto the table.

'Chocolate!' They chorused.

'With tea, proper tea,' Marta decided. Shunning the instant coffee and the milk, she found glasses, made drinks with sliced lemon and sugar.

Marta climbed quickly out of bed. The air was nippy and goose pimples rashed her arms. Rosa had been happy then, she thought, that Easter morning. I could write maybe, tell her family about that. Her kindness, buying us treats and re-creating a little piece of home.

* * *

Richard tried not to be distracted by the skimpily dressed girl giving it her all on the pole. The rest of the club was deserted, plunged into gloom but the girl swayed in an isolated pool of light. Harper was watching from a table nearby. The place was chilly and the cold seemed to intensify the aroma of stale beer and cigarette smoke that the soft furnishings soaked up.

'Bit early, isn't it?' Richard drew up a chair beside Harper.

'Audition — we're one girl down.'

Richard gave him a look.

'The show goes on.' He was unapologetic.

'Lee Stone, your doorman — were you aware he had a criminal record?'

Harper shrugged.

'Car theft amongst other things. He's helping us now with our enquiries into the hit and run accident.'

Harper's attention shifted sharpish from the dancer to Richard. He frowned. 'You think Stone nicked my car?' Surprise was replaced by outrage as the full meaning hit home. 'I'll bloody have him . . . The bastard!' He ran a finger round the collar of his shirt.

'Any trouble between you?'

'Nothing that I was aware of. And I think I'd have known; he's not exactly subtle.'

'So why would he steal your car?'

The girl hooked one knee round the pole, arched backwards, her hair almost sweeping the floor, one hand running slowly from her collarbone, over her breasts and down to her thigh. Richard wrenched his gaze back to Harper.

'Search me. But if you do find out let me know, won't you?' He shook his head with disbelief. 'Bloody idiot.' He gestured to the dancer to stop. Moved to turn off the music. 'Thanks, love, I'll give you a bell.'

The girl nodded, wandered off to get dressed.

'I'd book her,' Richard muttered. He leafed back a couple of pages in his daybook, to the notes of Harper's first statement. 'Rosa didn't turn up for work on Monday. What about Stone?'

'It's his day off.'

'But they both worked Sunday?' Harper nodded.

'Anything going on between him and Rosa?'

'No, I'd have noticed. I don't like him round the girls.'

'Why's that, then?'

'Bit rough round the edges, nasty mouth on him. They shouldn't have to put up with that.'

'Anything physical?'

'Once or twice, harassment, copping a feel. I made it plain to him, any more of it and he'd be out.'

Richard nodded, wondering whether Stone's harassment had involved Rosa this time and whether it had got out of hand. Whether sexual assault had led to murder?

* * *

At the police station, introductions had been made for the tape and Janine and Butchers faced Stone and a duty solicitor across the table in interview room one.

Janine took in the truculent expression on Stone's face, the insolence in his watery blue eyes. He was a big man, solidly built, with the look of someone who could 'handle himself'. No match for a slender girl like Rosa.

'You work for Mr Harper,' Janine began. 'Why did you steal his car?'

'What car?' Playing innocent. His eyes mocking her. Janine changed tack. 'Tell me about Rosa Milicz?'

'What about her?'

'You like her?'

'Not especially.'

'Why's that? She turn you down?'

Stone sneered. 'No.'

Janine sensed the question rankled. She could feel the anger not far below the surface. Like many of the violent men she had dealt with, Stone had a short fuse and his aggression belied an insecurity that made him quick to respond to imagined slights or insults.

'Mr Harper doesn't trust you with the girls.'

'What! A gentleman like me!' He swung his neck this way and that as he mocked offence. The gesture reminded Janine of the dances of the rap artists Michael used to like; that male posturing, the come and get me pose.

'When did you last see Rosa?'

'Sunday. At work.'

'Did you ever have a relationship with her?'

'I prefer my brunettes with bigger tits.' He leered pointedly at Janine.

Prat. She hoped he could read the cold loathing in her expression.

Butchers shifted uncomfortably.

'Let's go over everything very slowly again,' she said, 'just in case you missed something.'

An hour and a half later, Stone had maintained his brash front and they all needed a break.

In the corridor outside Butchers sighed loudly. 'What about the witness?' he suggested.

It was a good idea. If the witness could identify Stone and Gleason as the men she'd seen running from the blazing car, Janine would have stronger grounds for further interviews.

'Get them in this afternoon if possible,' Janine told him. 'Book the ID suite.'

Butchers nodded and set off, looking a little happier now he had a mission.

'Boss,' one of the DCs approached and handed her a document with a note attached. These told her that dental records in Poland matched their victim. The dead woman was one Rosa Milicz, believed to be living with family members on the outskirts of Krakow. Least we know we're talking about the right person now, she thought. She told the officer to arrange for the Polish authorities to make sure any family were formally notified.

Shap came out of interview room two, where he'd been talking to Gleason. He looked fed up.

'Well?' Janine asked him.

'Off-pat but he's shaking. Yours?'

'Cocky. Can I?'

Inside the room Shap updated the tape and sat back with his arms folded, happy to let Janine have a crack.

'I've just been having a very interesting talk with Lee Stone,' she told Gleason, who was rubbing at his long face repeatedly and whose body odour tainted the air. 'He's been very helpful.'

Gleason kept quiet.

'Bit of a chequered past, Lee Stone. Now you, you've never been in prison: suspended sentence, community service order. We see that a lot, you know, associates who get dragged into things, get out of their depth. What can you tell us about yesterday morning?'

'Nothing,' he said urgently.

'The car, the little girl?'

'I don't know what you're on about.' He bit at his thumb nail.

Janine waited a moment, studying him. 'That little girl died last night. We won't stop till we've got a conviction. Case like this — feelings run high.'

Gleason swallowed, his Adam's apple large on his scrawny neck.

'Half eight, nine a.m. where were you?' Shap asked.

'Home.'

'We've already got one witness,' Janine pointed out, 'saw you and Lee Stone running from the car. And there'll be others. Evidence too, on the car, in the car.'

'People make that mistake: fire, think it all goes up in smoke but the technology we've got now — fantastic.' Shap sounded positively delirious.

Gleason's eyes swerved between the pair of them, he brought his arms across his chest. Defensive, Janine thought, hiding, protecting. He scratched at his forearm.

'Who was driving?' Janine said sharply.

The scratching stopped. 'No comment,' Gleason said, a waver in his voice.

Sod it. Janine rolled her eyes at Shap. The 'no comment' told her two things: Gleason had something to hide and they would not get anything else out of him now.

* * *

Butchers stared at the woman. He couldn't believe he was hearing this. It was all arranged, she was their best hope, and now she was standing there, her eyes shifty, face twitching, telling him she was pulling out.

'All you have to do is look through the glass. See if the men you saw are there.'

She shook her head, moved as if to go inside.

'You were happy to help us yesterday. Has someone been getting at you?'

She blinked rapidly, locked him with a defiant stare. 'No. I just don't want to get involved.'

'But the little girl . . .' He could barely contain the sense of righteous anger mounting inside him. She had to help them. She had to.

She shook her head, refusing to listen and shut the door.

Butchers stood there, his jaw tight, his hands clenched, his breathing ragged. Across the waste ground the sky arced, a canvas of heavy clouds interrupted here and there by shafts of vibrant sunlight. She'd seen it all from here, Butchers thought, a clear view across to where the car had been left. And now? Had she got kids? He wanted to bray on the door again, drag her out and force her into his car. He waited long enough and then, feeling sick, turned to go.

* * *

'I had to release them,' Janine told him when he reported to her office. 'Without that witness . . .'

'Changed her mind,' he laughed harshly. 'Had it changed for her, more like.'

Shap nodded in agreement.

'But they're good for it,' Butchers insisted. 'They were seen leaving the car.' He was agitated, reluctant to accept the situation.

'By a witness who won't stand up,' she said emphatically. 'We need something stronger. We'll keep tabs on them, a couple of DCs round the clock, and keep digging. Pull them back in as soon as we've a stronger case. We're getting wall to wall press coverage and I'm sure we'll get more people coming forward.'

'But, Boss . . .'

'That's the way it is, Butchers. Deal with it.' She was surprised at his pushing it. He knew the rules.

'Now I'm going to pay a call on the Chinleys, later.' She paused, looking from one of them to the other by way of invitation. Shap avoided eye contact, Butchers showed willing. ''Bout five thirty,' she told him. 'Come and find me.'

* * *

The remaining couple of hours flew by as she read reports from the teams on the cases and double checked that she'd recorded everything she had to in her case-book.

She was almost ready to leave when Richard arrived back from the Topcat Club.

'Harper wasn't best pleased to learn Stone is down for nicking his car,' he said.

'But he didn't put Rosa and Stone together?'

Richard shook head. 'And no one else did either.'

Janine groaned. 'It's like juggling soot.'

'Welcome back.'

She rocked her head from side to side, trying to ease the tension in her neck. 'I've done a day's work before I clock on. I knew I'd be stretched but I didn't expect it to be quite so full on so soon.'

He smiled. 'How about dinner,' he said, 'my treat? Next evening we get free.'

Oh, God. She hadn't the energy. Any free evenings were for chores and kids and collapsing — not sparkling conversation and long, leisurely meals.

'Richard, thanks. But . . . you'd have to stab me with a fork just to keep me awake. My biggest ambition is eight hours unbroken sleep . . . six,' she amended. 'I'll let you know when she starts sleeping through.' She smiled as she opened her office door. 'Took Tom three years.' She laughed at the ripple of exasperation that crossed his face.

CHAPTER EIGHT

The Chinleys lived in a neat brick terraced house a few minutes' walk from Oak Lane school. They were attractive properties with generous sized rooms, stained glass in the windows, wooden porches overhanging the front door and small gardens back and front. Janine and Pete had almost bought one on the adjoining street but the sale had fallen through and they'd ended up buying something bigger a few months later when the death of Pete's father meant they could afford a bigger deposit. These terraces were selling for a small ransom nowadays as more and more professionals looked for housing in the area.

Debbie and Chris Chinley both came to the door. Debbie seemed tinier than ever, made frail by grief, like a damaged bird. Chris looked remote, his eyes never really focusing on the here and now.

Their living room was adorned with photos of Ann-Marie. Their only child.

'I'm so sorry,' Janine said. You could never say it enough. Not for something like this. Butchers nodded his own condolences.

'Thanks for your flowers,' Debbie said, her voice light, brittle. 'Everybody's been brilliant — really. And school . . .' she struggled.

There was an awkward pause.

'You got the car?' Chris Chinley asked.

'Yes,' Janine replied, 'it's with forensics now. We're talking to people who saw the vehicle and I think we're making progress.'

'Meaning?' he asked bitterly.

'Chris, don't,' Debbie said.

'We have some very promising leads,' Janine tried to reassure him.

'You know who it was?' he demanded. His broad, swarthy face darkening, his short, dark lashes flickering rapidly over his eyes.

Janine held up her hands, shaking her head. 'I can't talk to you about that,' she said gently.

'It doesn't change anything,' Debbie said simply. 'If you convict them — she's still . . .' She took a deep breath. 'I want something good to come from this . . .'

Chris sprang to his feet, headed out of the room. Janine signalled for Butchers to follow. 'I keep forgetting,' Debbie said. 'How daft is that? I keep thinking where's Ann-Marie, is she in her room, or I'd better get her dance kit ready and then I remember. Over and over.'

Janine nodded. All she could do was listen, sit there and listen and thank God that she wasn't Debbie Chinley.

* * *

Chris Chinley paced the kitchen looking out of place. Too raw for the neat white and jade units, the grey marble worktop and the fridge with its assortment of magnets.

'Something good,' he mimicked, 'what possible good . . . that bastard is out there . . . drawing breath.' He paused rubbing his large hands over his face, over the stubble and the shadows that made his eyes appear sunken.

The dog under the table raised its head and gave a whine. Chinley ignored it.

He spoke again. 'You lot talk about promising leads and making progress.'

'It's not just talk,' Butchers insisted.

'You've got him?' Butchers saw the hope flare in Chinley's eyes. 'Where is he? At the station?'

If only! Butchers looked away, his jaw clenched, betraying his own frustration. Stone should have been locked up tight and waiting for due process to kick in. There were times when he loathed the constraints of the job, the way the scallies played the system and won. Times when he felt screwed by the rules and regulations and the cowardice of the great British public who banged on endlessly about crime but ran a mile if they were asked to help do anything about it.

Chinley rounded on him, appalled. 'Still out there?' Almost a whisper, his arm pointing, his face vivid with disbelief. 'Still out there?' he repeated.

Butchers swallowed, felt a wave of shame. This man deserved better.

'Who is he?' Chinley moved closer to Butchers. 'Who is it? Who killed my Ann-Marie?'

Butchers shook his head; he felt the sweat break out on his upper body, his heartbeat sprint.

'Please?' Chinley whispered, his eyes locked onto Butchers', eyes spiked with pain.

* * *

Janine wriggled out of her coat in the hall. Eleanor appeared from the front room.

'How was school?' Janine asked as they went along the hallway.

''Kay. I got an A in geography.'

'Well done, Ellie.'

'And Naomi's having a sleepover — can I go?'

'Yes, 'course you can.'

'Cool.' Eleanor produced her mobile phone and turned, heading upstairs accompanied by bleats and beeps as she called her friend.

In the kitchen-cum-living room, Pete was flying Charlotte around like a plane; she was shrieking with glee. 'Approaching runway two. Clear for landing Charlie Lima.'

'Don't you get enough of that at work?' Janine said.

'Give me a go,' Tom yelled. 'It's my turn.'

Janine held out her hands and took the baby, settled her on one hip. 'Have you been flying? Clever girl.'

Pete bent to lift Tom. And raised him up.

Michael came in with a pile of dirty pots which he began to put in the dishwasher. Another year and a half and Michael would be off to university, leaving home maybe. Though more of them seemed to stay put than they had in Janine's time; chose courses close to the family nest. Money perhaps. She and Pete should be able to help him out with fees and the like so if he wanted to go further afield then the opportunity would be there.

'Parents' evening.' Michael took a bite of an apple and handed Janine a letter from his sixth-form college. 'Next week.'

'Going all right?' Sometimes she felt she barely saw him these days. Probably healthy, growing up, gaining his independence.

'Yes, good.'

'Great. Don't know whether it'll be me or your dad but one of us will be there.'

Charlotte began to grizzle. 'You hungry?' Janine took a bottle from the fridge and put it in the warmer. Charlotte screeched.

'Did you get them Mum?' Tom held his arms out rigid as Pete placed him back on the floor. 'Did you put them in jail?'

'Not yet,' she said. 'Doing my best, though.'

* * *

The streets were slick with rain, reflecting light from the lamp-posts and car headlights. Chris's chest felt tight, hard. As though he had swallowed cement and it had gradually set, swelling and stiffening. His heart was a boulder, lodged like a weight in the centre of him.

He imagined the bastards' faces, the surprise when they clocked who he was. His grief releasing him to do whatever he chose. A rock smashing into them, crushing the fingers that had steered the wheel, the feet that had gunned the accelerator, blowing them away . . . He braked sharply. No point being caught for speeding before he'd had his chance.

Chris had never been much of a fighter. At school, his big build and his easy-going nature had spared him the attention of the hard cases. The one time he had got mixed up in a playground brawl, he'd decked one of the ringleaders and received a broken nose for his pains.

Later, as a man, the only fights he'd known were times he'd intervened in drunken mêlées. One time, three lads were kicking seven shades of shit out of another man. Chris had pulled them off, yelling that the police were coming. He got a shove or two and a load of abuse but the trio legged it. The broken nose helped. Made Chris look like a boxer. Another time, he'd got mixed up in a lovers' fight. The man had been slapping the woman about the head, hard enough to break her jaw. 'Leave her be,' Chris had told him, one hand raised in warning. 'That's way out of order.'

The man had turned to Chris and let go of the girl. Released, she flew at Chris. 'Get off him,' she shrieked, oblivious to the fact that Chris hadn't laid a finger on the guy, 'yer wanker, eff off.' And she had clouted Chris with her handbag then kicked out at him with one vicious looking stiletto which raked a neat quarter-inch furrow down his shin.

Now he wasn't frightened or agitated because it was like he was on automatic. He imagined that soldiers maybe felt like that before battle or someone jumping out of a plane.

He knew the way. He'd done a few jobs on one of the estates on the fringe of Wythenshawe. Sort of places people bought because it was near the airport and the motorways. They wouldn't be there more than a few years and they could buy it newly built and sell it for a neat profit and it even came painted, carpeted and fully fitted. Move in a couch and a bed and you were in business.

The address he was making for was less desirable. Council flat in the worst part. No one here ever rang a plumber; under the tenancy agreements they'd all be fixed up by direct works, or they wouldn't — depending on who you talked to. Regular items in the free newspapers featured scenes of council tenants pointing to leaking pipes, giant field mushrooms on the wall and sodden carpets.

* * *

She'd just finished feeding Charlotte and Pete had his coat on and was kissing the baby goodbye when Richard rang. 'Bad news. Stone and Gleason, obbos have lost them.'

'They've lost them! Shit!' She flushed with irritation. 'Circulate descriptions to all patrols. Get Butchers and Shap and anyone else you can pull in on standby, we'd better bloody well find them. Keep me informed.'

Tom picked up on the language like a shot. 'Aw! Mum said the s-word and the b-word.'

'How did they lose them?'

'They were on foot, our lads were following but they weren't quick enough. Stone and Gleason gave them the slip. There's more,' Richard added.

'What more?' Her voice dangerous.

Richard exhaled. 'Chris Chinley was seen in the area around the same time.'

'What!' she snapped. 'You are joking!'

Pete raised Charlotte high. 'Houston,' he said, 'we have a problem.'

* * *

Butchers and Shap waited in the car. They had driven round in circles looking for signs of the missing men but seen nothing.

Shap was bored, shifting in his seat and sighing loudly. Butchers was tight-lipped; he started when the radio crackled. 'Two men answering descriptions of suspects seen on Bradbury Road, near Halton Lane junction, heading west.'

Butchers started the car. 'Unit responding.' It was five minutes away. Butchers made it in three. The location was deserted, amber streetlights reflecting off broken pavements. Small houses, curtains drawn and locked up tight. Everyone in safe behind closed doors.

'Get a closer look.' Butchers said unbuckling his seat belt.

'What's the point?' Shap asked him. 'They'll be long gone.'

'You coming or not?' Butchers snarled.

'Not,' Shap retorted, folding his arms and wriggling down in his seat.

Butchers slammed the car door, fastened his coat against the rain, switched on his torch and walked along the street. Once there had been a parade of shops but a combination of vandalism and poverty had forced most of them to close. Nowhere now to get a carton of milk or a packet of fags. Butchers walked round the block and back. He could smell curry from somewhere and for a moment he thought about getting a take-away. There was a place back towards town — Chinese. It was hours since he'd eaten.

On the side road he saw movement, a dog? No, a fox. The distinctive tail, the rusty colouring. He smiled. The animal slipped out of view into some sort of an alleyway. Butchers crossed over and followed, the beam of his torch picking out steps. Not an alleyway but an old subway tunnel. He wondered why they'd built it here, something to do with the warehouses across the way, or the railways. He went down the steps, played the light into the subway.

He could see the fox ahead; the animal hesitated at a heap of rubbish by the far steps, glanced at Butchers and then back at the rubbish, reluctant to leave. But as Butchers drew closer the animal skittered away up the far steps. Butchers swung his torch over the rubbish. His heart juddered, his hand began to tremble, the yellow light of the ray jouncing up and down, erratically.

'Oh, sweet Jesus,' he prayed. 'Oh, no. No,' as he stared at the crumpled figure, the clothes. The dark mess, the slick pool on the floor. Jeremy Gleason. With half his head blown off.

CHAPTER NINE

The Press had got wind of a fresh kill and Janine was temporarily blinded by the barrage of bright flashes from the cameras. She skirted the crowd and ignored the clamour for comments.

It was cold enough for gloves but she had to peel her own off and flex her fingers into thin plastic ones. She already wore a protective suit over her trousers and now she pulled the top of it over her arms and zipped it up. The scene of crime manager signed her in and she edged past the gantry of lights that were illuminating the steps leading down to where the body lay.

The sight made her recoil in shock, though anyone looking would only have noticed a sharp intake of breath and a tightening around the jaw. She looked at the mess around the man, the copious amount of blood and gore, the position he lay in, one leg flung out from his body, the thin pale ankle showing between his sock and his trousers, a fake Rolex on one wrist still ticking away. She felt a wave of sadness, too, that a life should end this way, suddenly, savagely, in a disused subway.

Richard stood beside her. 'Gunshot wound to the head,' he said grimly, 'they've not found the weapon. And no sign of Lee Stone — he's not been back to the flat.'

'Maybe I should have hung on to Gleason — gone for broke. If letting him go led to . . .' she broke off. She recalled the fear in Gleason's eyes when she had questioned him. She had assumed that he'd been fearful of the police but maybe there'd been more to it. Frightened of Stone, too?

'We don't know that,' Richard said. 'We've no idea what's behind this.'

'We need to find Stone,' she said decisively. 'Get a team onto likely haunts, friends and family. And put out a bulletin. But warn the public not to approach him, he's probably armed.' She hugged herself, tucking her hands under her arms in an effort to keep warm.

Richard stood aside as another piece of the forensic kit was brought through. 'If this is Stone's doing, what's his motive?'

'Stop Gleason talking? He was shaky when we had him in.'

'Talking about the hit and run? Or he knew something about Rosa?'

'Take your pick.'

'If Stone did both killings,' Richard spoke slowly, testing his thoughts, 'they've got very different MOs. Here we've got a shooting and no attempt to hide the body. With Rosa we've strangulation and then efforts to disguise her.'

She thought about it. 'Maybe because he had different motives?'

'OK. With Rosa — he blows his cool and kills her when she rejects him, whatever . . .'

'And this is more like an execution.'

'There is someone else — with a cast-iron motive. Chris Chinley. We know he was in the vicinity.'

Janine's stomach clenched. 'How did Chris Chinley know who our suspects were?' she asked sharply.

Richard raised his eyebrows.

'Unless a little bird told him?' Janine said, thinking of the visit to the Chinleys — of how Chris had stormed out followed by Butchers. 'In which case, I'll ring its flamin' neck.'

She looked back at what was left of Jeremy Gleason. The technicians were taking measurements and videoing the scene. The atmosphere was calm and methodical, nothing that reflected the urgency that batted away in her own chest, or the panic that must have filled this man's last few seconds.

'We can't do much more here, now,' she told Richard. 'We'd better see whether Chris Chinley's at home.'

Dread settled like lead in Janine's guts as they drove round to the house. If Chris had done this the repercussions would be enormous. She could understand his fury, the pain that the men who had taken his precious little girl were not yet behind bars, but to act on that . . . had he even considered what it would do to Debbie? To lose Ann-Marie and then Chris? Because no matter how much the public might sympathise with a grieving father, there was no way on earth that deliberate revenge killing could be exonerated. Chris would do time. And what did it say about his faith in Janine, in her team? He hadn't even trusted them to do their job. She felt sick.

* * *

Debbie opened the door to Janine and Richard, waving them in past the plethora of flowers, cards and teddies from well-wishers.

'I'm sorry to call so late,' Janine told her.

'Has something happened?'

Janine avoided answering. 'Actually, we need a word with Chris. Is he in?'

'Why?' Debbie's face seemed to sharpen with trepidation. 'What is it?'

Chris appeared in the kitchen doorway.

'Just routine.' Richard said.

Janine regarded Chris, his face set, eyes glittery — with what? Fatigue or grief or guilt? She turned back to Debbie. 'Could you give us a moment?'

'Routine?' Debbie asked. 'What do you mean? Have you caught them?' Anticipation made her voice rise.

'No. Chris?' Janine invited the man to collude with her, to reassure Debbie, tell her he was happy to see the police on his own.

He raised his chin. 'I haven't got anything to hide.'

Debbie frowned, looked from one to another.

'This isn't easy,' said Janine.

Chris stood immovable, his arms folded tightly across his chest, lips a thin line, his nostrils dilated, edged in white, revealing his pent-up tension.

Richard exhaled noisily. 'Earlier this evening you were seen in Northern Moor. On Moorlands Road. Could you tell me what you were doing there?'

'Just driving.'

'Why there?' Janine asked him. He said nothing. 'What time did you get back?'

Chris simply stared at her, his eyes feverish.

'What's going on?' Debbie demanded.

Janine paused, giving Chris a final chance to ask for privacy, but he stood his ground. 'In the course of the enquiry we were able to identify two suspects,' she said calmly. 'They were being kept under observation. They live in Moorlands Road. Now one of them has been killed.'

Debbie gasped. Looked to her husband.

'Well, it wasn't me!' he burst out.

'You were seen,' said Richard.

'I was there, yes, I went to the flat. I never got out of the car.'

'Who told you?' Janine asked. Silence.

'You just sat in the car?'

'Where the hell would I get a gun from, anyway?' He flung his arms wide.

'Who said it was a gun?' Janine's heart kicked in her chest. Had he given himself away?

'It's been on the radio. A man with gunshot wounds. When you said — that's him, isn't it?'

He could be telling the truth. How she hoped he was. But she could no longer take his word at face value. She had to set aside any personal connection and retreat into formality. Do her job, and be seen to do it. 'Will you be prepared to take a gunshot residue test and provide your clothing for forensic examination?'

'And if I don't?' he said bitterly.

Oh, please, Janine thought, don't make this any worse than it already is.

* * *

They were alone at last. Chris couldn't bear Debbie's eyes on him. Huge, intense, as if they would suck the truth from his bones. Blaming him, accusing him.

'What the hell were you thinking of?' she whispered. 'How could you?' She took a step forward, her head inclined, a frown puckered across her brow.

He jerked his body away, heat surged down his forearms and into his fists. He balled them tight, felt the tremors that ran along his jaw, through his tongue.

'Me?' He wanted to rail at her. 'That's bloody rich. What about you? If you . . .' He didn't say it. Bit down hard and said nothing. Speech was a weapon.

She began to cry; little snuffling sounds. 'Tell me you didn't do anything. You didn't, did you?'

You stupid bitch, he thought. As if I'd tell you — and then listen while you told the world and looked for something good to come of it.

'Chris, talk to me, please. Say something.'

He shook his head. He didn't know the way back from this island of rage. Didn't want to find one. The anger was keeping him alive, making him strong.

His girl was gone. He recalled Ann-Marie's hand curled loose in his own. Round and round the garden like a teddy bear. Tiny nails, translucent. He turned to the door. Debbie moved after him. Don't touch me, he prayed, don't lay a finger on me.

'It won't bring her back,' she shouted.

I didn't let her go, he thought. Don't blame me, not for any of this. If you'd just held her hand. You should have held her hand. He left the room, the words banging like a chant in his head. You should have held her hand.

* * *

Jeremy Gleason's next of kin was his mother who lived at an address in one of the poorer areas of Old Trafford.

Janine went to tell her the news.

'Who is it?' The woman yelled through the front door, unwilling to open it at such a late hour.

'Police,' Janine answered.

Before she could offer to post her proof of ID there was the sound of locks being drawn back. Mrs Gleason opened the door.

'Now what's he done?' She demanded. Her face was furrowed with lines; they radiated from her thin mouth, fanned her eyes and scored across her forehead. Pouches of dark skin hung beneath her eyes. She had brassy golden hair and wore a cheap, blue, velour lounging-suit and a red plaid dressing gown. Janine noticed bare feet with orange nail polish.

'Can I come in a minute?'

The woman stepped back and let her in. 'Always in trouble, always,' Mrs Gleason continued, her voice high and brittle, as she led Janine into a small sitting room awash with Oriental bric-a-brac. The telly was on, the volume muted. 'The times I've had you lot round. In the end I told 'em, I can't do anything with him. He's not bad — he's just stupid. Born stupid.'

'Mrs Gleason,' Janine stopped her. 'Please sit down. I'm afraid I've got some very bad news.'

The woman froze. She opened her mouth, and then closed it again. Sat unsteadily on the sofa. Janine watched her hand grip the edge of the seat cushion.

'I got a phone call this evening, a man had been found. He'd been shot.'

Mrs Gleason stared at her, her pupils huge, her mouth trembling.

'I'm so very sorry.'

'You sure?'

'It's Jeremy.'

Mrs Gleason shook her head; her brow creased even more deeply, her eyes filled with tears. She looked up at the ceiling, wrapped her arms about herself.

Janine took in the clutch of family photos on a shelf: Mrs Gleason and another woman, a sister perhaps; one of Jeremy at a wedding, lanky and grinning; one of him with a child, a little boy. His child?

'Why?' The woman asked her.

'We don't know.'

Now wasn't the time to tell her the police had been talking to her son in connection with a crime.

Mrs Gleason pressed her hand to her mouth and squeezed her eyes tight shut.

'Can I get you a drink?' Janine asked her.

'There's a bottle of Bailey's in the kitchen, second cupboard.'

Janine retrieved it and poured a generous measure into a glass. Mrs Gleason took it and drank half of it in one go. Janine could smell the sweet blend of liqueur and cream.

She looked at Janine; her face started to crumple. 'What do I do now? I don't know . . . what happens?'

Gently, Janine talked her through the immediate necessities. Was Jeremy married, had he any family of his own?

'Divorced,' his mother said, 'that's his lad.' She tilted her glass at the photograph. 'He hasn't seen him for a while.'

Janine explained that there would be no need to start funeral arrangements as a post-mortem would have to be carried out and nothing could happen until the coroner released the body.

Mrs Gleason seemed to take most of it in. 'Does Lee know?' she said suddenly. 'Lee Stone, he was living at Lee's.'

'Not yet. We haven't been able to speak to Lee, he's not at home. If he gets in touch with you will you please let us know? He's wanted for questioning.'

Confusion and then distress flashed across her face. 'Oh, God,' she began as she realised the implication.

'We don't know what happened,' Janine told her clearly. 'We've no idea at the moment. But Lee was with Jeremy shortly before he was found — we really need to talk to him.'

There was a pause and Mrs Gleason took another drink from her glass.

'Would you like me to arrange for someone to come and sit with you?' Janine offered.

The woman shook her head. 'Our Karen's just down the road, I'll go to hers.'

'I'll wait while you call her.'

As Janine watched her make the call she wondered about Rosa Milicz's family — who had broken the news to them, how much had they been told? Rosa would probably have been sending money home to them; did they know she'd been an exotic dancer or had she pretended she was doing something more respectable? The wages she earned in the UK would have made life better for them all and then, out of nowhere, someone had strangled her, mutilated her and thrown her in the river. Why? Why Rosa? Why Gleason?

CHAPTER TEN

Towards morning Janine dreamed that Ann-Marie was lying in the road and Janine couldn't rouse her. She realised with a sense of horror that the child was dead. She felt a twist of guilt. It was her fault. They'd find out. Panic skewed inside her. She turned to see a row of people watching her; they looked angry. Then the child had gone and in her place was Rosa Milicz; someone had shot her. There was the noise then. Janine ducked. She reared awake to the sound of Charlotte crowing. The picture of the dream evaporating as she tried to clutch at it. Had Rosa had a face? How had she known it was Rosa?

Getting up, Janine looked in the cot. Charlotte greeted her with a little shriek.

'Good morning,' Janine rubbed the baby's stomach. 'Aren't you lovely,' she told her. 'Yes, you are. My best girl.'

* * *

There was an edgy mood in the incident room that morning. The banter a little too savage, the laughter forced. As soon as she began to speak the team were made unequivocally aware of Janine's ire. She could have been reading a shopping list and they'd still have got the message. The boss was steaming. She tapped the edge of Jeremy Gleason's photograph. 'He was a suspect in the death by reckless driving of a seven-year-old. He may also have been able to help us with the murder of Rosa Milicz.' She paused, scanned the room. Took in Butchers avoiding eye contact, hunched in his seat. As well he might.

She carried on, her voice quieter which only emphasised the contained fury. 'Someone on this team leaked crucial identifying information to a man half-deranged with grief. We don't know yet who pulled the trigger on Jeremy Gleason but, whether or not it was Chris Chinley, I will never accommodate such a serious breach of discipline.' She looked from one officer to another, insisting that they share her frustration. 'We are a team. A stunt like this reflects on every other person in this room. There's only one side — you're on it or you're out. I expect whoever jeopardised this investigation to have the basic bloody guts to own up. You know where my office is.'

She stepped back, folded her arms and leant against a desk, her eyes still roving the room, taking in the discomfort that rippled through the group.

Richard took over. 'OK, three cases — we'll take new information on them one by one. Jeremy Gleason, murder. Pathology has promised an initial report first thing after lunch. At this point in time we're looking at Chris Chinley and Lee Stone. Chris Chinley has agreed to a gunshot residue test and his clothes are with the lab. He was in the area, intending to go after Gleason and Stone. Claims he bottled out.' He shrugged; the jury was still out on that one. 'All forces are on lookout for Lee Stone and we are calling on family and known associates and checking places he may have holed up.' Officers nodded, exchanged glances, scribbled notes.

'Prior to this, we know Stone and Gleason were mates. Maybe they quarrelled or maybe Stone took him out because he knew too much. And remember, although we have no other suspects at present, enquiries might turn up someone new. Talk to Gleason's other pals, neighbours, family — did Gleason have any enemies we should know about?

'Next case — Rosa Milicz — murder. The DNA profile from the material under her nails should be back tomorrow. At that point we can run it against Stone and Gleason. Rosa's relatives have been notified. Enquiries are ongoing at the club. So far all we're getting is a load of no's: no boyfriend, no trouble, no dodgy clients, no address. Rosa was an illegal immigrant, the rest of the girls are kosher — though the filing system leaves something to be desired. Now Rosa was Polish and so is the club owner, Konrad Sulikov. Possibly a connection there. We're doing a paper search on him. One big gap is her address — someone must know where she was living but we haven't got to them yet. We're still no nearer a crime scene for the murder.' The yellow pins had spread along the meandering route of the river showing more areas searched and ruled out. 'Every crime scene tells a story: who was there, who did what to whom. Without it, to be frank, we're struggling. We're redoubling efforts to find Rosa's home in the hope that'll lead us to the scene.'

Richard turned back to the boards. 'We want to talk to Lee Stone about this one as well. He worked at the club, he was the doorman. A search has been made of Stone's flat but that's not our scene.'

'He liked to mess about with the dancers, trying it on.' Shap put in.

'Yes and he's a history of sexual violence. But there is no prior relationship between Stone and Rosa. Not that we can find.'

Richard moved over to the picture of Ann-Marie, the details of the Mercedes. 'Finally, the hit and run. Now death due to dangerous driving plus failing to stop etc. etc. Here we have sightings of the Merc and there's a pattern emerging with the odd rogue report that is out of sync.' He pointed to a time that was outside the accepted parameters. 'Where's that, Butchers?'

Butchers started, stumbled over his words. 'Erm . . . Burnage at ten to eight.'

'That Mercedes will have been everywhere from Land's End to John O'Groats before we're done,' said Richard. 'The fire damage to the car means we've not got anything concrete from forensics yet to place Stone or Gleason behind the wheel. They're still on the job; all we need is an eyelash, a speck of dandruff. The chances might be slim but stranger things have happened.'

Shap tapped his pen against his notebook. 'We've had a couple more witnesses come forward and they are all singing from the same song sheet — describing Stone and Gleason near where the car was dumped.' It was good news, reinforcing the likelihood of being able to hold Stone for questioning when he was finally found.

'CCTV?' Richard asked.

The officers reviewing tapes from service stations in a forty mile radius shook their heads — nothing as yet.

Janine spoke out. 'Stone's the key — those of you with sources put the word out. Bring him in.' She left the room briskly. A collective sigh of relief followed her departure though people were then quick to move on to their own particular tasks, anxious to escape the prevailing awkward atmosphere. And no one wanted to speak to Butchers.

* * *

Richard asked Shap to stay behind. Edged him over to the far corner out of earshot.

'We all know who it is, Shap. Body language screaming guilty as hell. Can't you have a quiet word with him?'

Shap was silent. His expression guarded.

'She won't let it rest, you know. And neither will I.'

'I'm not with you, sir,' Shap said coldly, 'is that all?' He cocked his head.

Richard gave a shrug of resignation. Shap was keeping mum — so be it.

* * *

The Lemon wanted his piece of the action. Some things never change, thought Janine as she stood in his office, concentrating on an ancient picture of the Queen from the 1950s that had pride of place on his wall.

'You trying for some sort of record?' Hackett said. 'One suspect dead, another AWOL and the grieving father in the frame for the shooting because your team's leaking like a sieve.'

'I'm dealing with it, sir.'

'How exactly? If the press get hold of this . . .'

'They won't. I had no alternative; I had no grounds to hold those men any longer.' She defended her decision.

'And the leak? Discipline — if you lose that . . . Come down and come down hard.'

'The team know how things stand. I'll be dealing with the culprit this afternoon.'

'Who is it?'

'I've got a pretty clear idea but until I've spoken to the officer directly . . .' She'd do this by the book.

'Demotion? Suspension?'

'I'll make that decision when I have all the facts.' And it'd be a damn shame. Butchers was a reliable copper. Had been up till now. Then what? Meltdown. Such a waste.

'If they think you're a soft touch . . .'

Janine recalled the reactions in the incident room. 'Hardly.'

'Not the most auspicious return to duty.' Hackett observed. 'Maybe I should have let Mayne lead. Give you time to . . . readjust.'

Janine was determined not to rise to the bait; nothing he liked more than a sniping match; when things got tough he invariably took to undermining those junior to him. The old school approach.

'If we're finished here, sir, I've got a lot to do,' she said brightly. He nodded reluctantly and she escaped.

* * *

One of the clients had a paper. POLICE IDENTIFY ROSA was splashed across the front, *Murder Victim Polish.* Marta's heart thumped when she saw it and she stifled the urge to exclaim. She longed to read more, hoping that the man would leave it in the lounge when he went in with Zofia. Rosa used to pore over the free newspaper that got delivered. She'd pick out words that she didn't know and look them up in her little dictionary. Lots weren't in it and she'd have to figure them out from the context.

But the man tucked it into his coat and Marta didn't get a chance. She would have to try and catch the news on the television. The men liked to have it on while they waited.

Now the police knew it was Rosa would they come here? She would talk to the others, they would have to be very careful, more so than usual.

Marta thought about the baby. Rosa had chattered about names late one night when she got in. 'It's due in August,' she had said. 'If it's a girl I will call her after you.'

Marta had wrinkled her nose, waved away the idea. 'I never liked my name.' She had leaned forward, sliding a cigarette from the packet. Begun to speak carefully, 'And Rosa, you know . . .'

Rosa had flung her arm up in protest, no longer prepared to listen to reason. 'Don't! This is my baby, it's my life so just . . . *spierdalaj*,' she swore, 'fuck off and let me be.'

Now Marta went upstairs and sat on Rosa's bed and gazed out at the roofs through the grey net curtains. Rosa wasn't coming back. Rosa was gone. With her posture like a ballet dancer, that straight back and long neck, her luxurious dark hair.

Marta exhaled sharply. She got down on her knees and felt under the bed where she knew Rosa kept her bag. There were clothes and a couple of family photographs: people in their Sunday best. One was a church occasion, one of the brothers getting confirmed, Rosa had said. Marta peered at the Milicz clan. The father dead now. Here he looked like any family man. Rosa and her brothers wore bright smiles for the camera, their mother looked brittle, careworn. Also in the bag, there was a cloth wallet and inside it was the money that Rosa had been saving. Marta counted it. Just over £400. Most of her tips had been sent back home. Marta put the cash in her own bag; no point in letting anyone else get their hands on it. It brought her £400 closer to a better life.

The doorbell rang and she smoothed her hair and adjusted her skirt as she went back downstairs to work.

CHAPTER ELEVEN

Every case generated a phenomenal amount of paperwork. As officer in charge, Janine not only had to keep tabs on all the different elements of the investigation and see their reports but also keep a meticulous log of her own and ensure that there were no omissions which could later jeopardise the chance of a result. She was multi-tasking, sifting through her in-tray and trying for some sort of prioritisation and also reading her emails when she was interrupted by Shap. 'Boss, you got a minute, it's about Ian . . .'

Still smarting from her encounter with Hackett, Janine felt her temper rise. 'He should be here — not you,' she said crisply, 'tell him to see me himself.'

'But, boss, it's just . . . he's straight as a die, everyone . . .'

'Shap, I'm not interested in excuses.'

'I just think, given the situation . . .'

'The situation,' she said hotly, 'is that he's a police officer—'

Shap interrupted. 'And his brother died in a hit and run and they never got anyone for it.'

'What?' Janine stared at him. 'Oh, God.' She shook her head and groaned. 'Where is he?'

'Outside, we're off to the Topcat now,' Shap said.

'He knows you're here?'

Shap gave a shake of his head.

'He should have told me,' Janine said. 'Why the hell didn't he tell me? None of this might have happened.'

Shap kept quiet.

'OK,' she told him by way of dismissal. 'Shap.'

He'd reached the door.

'You knew all along?'

Shap nodded.

'And did you talk to Ian about it, about maybe stepping down from the case?'

Shap fingered his neck, a sign of discomfort. 'I tried, he wasn't having it.'

'How hard did you try?'

'I mentioned it.' There was a defensive edge in his reply.

Janine could imagine. A word or two would probably be as far as a heart to heart went with these blokes. Was the younger generation any different? As Shap left, she thought of her son Michael; he wasn't at ease talking about anything that touched on emotional issues. He'd blush and mumble and generally squirm to be let off the hook. Some commentators now claimed the male brain was wired differently and others took that to mean there was no point in trying to change things. Janine didn't agree; she understood some of the consequences of emotional illiteracy. The men she most often hunted down could no more express their feelings than they could read and write. Illiterate on all counts.

* * *

Janine observed the post-mortem on Jeremy Gleason. Susan told her that the state of Gleason's head injury indicated a frontal shot from a relatively close distance. The angle of the entry wound suggested that the gun had been fired from above. The bullet had passed through Gleason's head and had been recovered from the floor of the tunnel. It would be sent to specialist services for identification.

'It fits with the location,' Janine said. 'The steps. If someone had fired at him from there.' She looked at his hands, the nails bitten down to the quick. Stupid not bad, his mother had said before she knew he was dead. Janine had got the same impression: Gleason had none of the guile or belligerence of Lee Stone.

How had Gleason reacted after the road accident? He had a child himself; had that prompted him to argue with Stone about whether they deny the crime? Or had he gone along with the plan willingly? Perhaps he'd lost his nerve later, after the men had been questioned? If the guilt about Ann-Marie's death had begun to prey on him, coupled with a fear that the police were onto them, he may have been thinking about confessing. Had Stone cottoned on and decided to save his own skin by silencing Gleason permanently? Or had an argument led to Stone pulling a gun on his friend? At the point where they had been seen leaving the flat — just before the police lost sight of them — there was no sign of coercion or aggression and certainly no weapons drawn.

'Nothing else to write home about,' Susan told her. 'Pretty straightforward.'

'Cause of death might be plain,' Janine said, 'whodunnit and why is anything but.'

There was an outside chance that Gleason's killing was linked to some other criminal activity that the police had yet to uncover. The drugs gangs in the city regularly settled disputes with a bullet. Except nothing ever remained settled. There'd be a drive-by or cycle-by shooting. And then a couple of weeks later another kid, almost always a black kid, would be gunned down in retaliation. Several times victims had been killed in error for other targets. Innocent bystanders caught up in the bloody and savage tit-for-tat. Janine had covered a couple of those cases. They'd been hard. Not only the tragic waste of young lives blown away but the sheer hopelessness of the gang members. Kids with deadly weapons and deader souls; trapped in a cycle of poverty, lawlessness and violence. Talking of honour and brotherhood. They had no hope or apparent desire for a life beyond the gang. After interviewing these boys, Janine had come away asking herself how it had come to this. How did babies, toddlers, youngsters grow up to be stone-cold killers, so completely alienated from the mainstream?

Janine considered the likelihood of a gang connection to the shooting but nothing they had learnt so far put Stone or Gleason anywhere close to that scene.

* * *

Harper was chatting to Andrea at one of the booths along the wall when Shap and Butchers arrived. He glanced up and pulled a weary face, got to his feet and met them halfway across the room. 'Back again?'

'There a problem?' said Shap.

'Just it's not very good for business. Word gets round.'

'That's the trouble with murder. Bloody inconvenient.'

'Well, have you any idea how long this is going to go on?' Harper's frustration was plain.

'Long as it takes.' Shap, followed by Butchers, continued over to join Andrea. Harper went behind the bar where the barmaid was re-stocking glasses and bottles, the clinking of the glasses audible above the soft, jazz music that was playing. Norah Jones begging someone to come away with her.

A flick of her eyes was all the greeting they got from Andrea. She lit a cigarette and sat back, left arm crossed over her waist acting as a prop for her other arm.

Shap dragged a chair over from a nearby table, turned it round, straddled it and nodded at the girl. Butchers sat down opposite her on the bench seat, pulling his daybook out and riffling through to the last entry.

'What do you make of Lee Stone?' Shap asked.

'Bad news. I never liked him. They reckon he shot that Gleason lad, don't they?' Her eyes sized Shap up, assessing whether the rumours were true.

'You ever come across Jeremy Gleason?' Butchers asked.

'Now and then. He hung about with Lee. I felt sorry for him really.'

'Why's that then?'

She shrugged. 'He was a bit of a loser that's all, like a big kid really. His eyes were out on stalks when he came in here — couldn't believe his luck.'

'He come in often?'

'No, couple of times, looking for Lee. Did Lee kill him?'

We don't know.'

'Tight that.'

'You saying you think he could have?' Shap said.

'I'm not saying owt, I'm asking.' She lowered her arm to the ashtray, flicked her thumbnail against the tip of the cigarette, dislodging the ash.

'Did Rosa ever have any bother with Stone?' said Shap.

'Don't think so, she stayed well clear, like the rest of us.'

'What about Sunday — you see him giving her any hassle? Making a nuisance of himself?'

'No.'

'But he did do that?'

'Don't you all?'

Shap grinned.

'You know she was pregnant?' Butchers put in.

Andrea grimaced, stopping mid-way through a toke on her fag. 'No. Oh, God.'

'Any idea who the father might be?'

Andrea shook her head.

'Anything else you can tell us?' Shap said.

'Like what?'

'Anything you might have remembered, anything sprung to mind?'

Andrea blew smoke out as she shook her head.

Shap nodded his thanks and Butchers checked his watch and noted the time in his book.

There were three other girls working: Shelley, Carmen and Dee. Shap and Butchers spoke to each of them and learnt nothing new. When they'd finished Butchers put his book and pen away slowly, eager to prolong the time away from the station but Shap caught his eye and jerked his head towards the exit. Time to face the music.

* * *

Debbie had gone quiet. Even her crying was silent. She'd been taking the tranquillisers that the doctor had prescribed. Other people had been in and out, making meals that neither of them could face, tidying up a bit and dealing with the demands of a world that still turned. Debbie was upstairs now, creeping about.

Chris sat in the kitchen, the television on, sound muted. Last night's Evening News was on the table, coverage of the accident on the front page. Ann-Marie's face, hair in bunches, her new front teeth looking big in her face. He wondered why they had chosen that photo rather than any other. They had hundreds of her, videos too: holidays, birthdays, Christmases. Would a day ever come when he could bear to see her on the screen, chattering and hamming it up for the camera? The way she put her hands on her hips when she was exasperated by something, the sudden gurgle in her laugh.

He turned the sound up as the lunchtime news came on and pressed record on the VCR. A picture flashed up, a mug shot. 'Greater Manchester police have taken the unusual step of issuing this picture of 27-year-old Lee Stone, who is wanted for questioning in connection with last night's shooting.' The shot changed to an alleyway and police tape fluttered in the wind. 'The victim, Jeremy Gleason, aged 24, died at the scene. Both men lived in the Wythenshawe area of Manchester.' The picture changed back to the studio. Behind the newsreader Stone's mug shot remained. 'Police have warned the public not to approach Lee Stone who may be armed but to contact the police immediately.'

And Ann-Marie? He was incensed. He killed my daughter too.

He fetched a bottle of vodka from the fridge and poured himself a tumbler full. He rewound the tape, played it again, freezing the image so he could study the photograph. Smoking steadily (no need to smoke in the garden now) he regarded the narrow eyes, the slight sneer to the mouth, the broad chin and close cut hair that gave Stone the look of a hard man, a bruiser.

Chris drank and smoked, replaying and freezing the tape each time the VCR switched back to standby. He swallowed and sucked until his mouth felt sour and his eyes ached. When he stood to go upstairs he stumbled and knocked the bottle and glass to the floor; they both smashed. He left them there.

Upstairs he peed but didn't bother to wash or clean his teeth. He went into Ann-Marie's room. The dog, lying on the lower bunk, lifted his head, looking wary, expecting to be banished.

Chris kicked off his trainers and pulled off his top and jeans. He lay down beside the dog and tugged at the purple 'groovy chick' duvet cover until it covered him and shut out the flat, grey light from the afternoon outside.

CHAPTER TWELVE

Butchers stood in front of Janine, eyes averted, hands clasped.

'Did you want to see Chris Chinley charged with murder? Does that make anything better? For them? For you?' There was a pause, his face remained impassive.

'You should have told me. You should never have been assigned to this case. Why didn't you say anything?' He didn't answer her, just stood there rocking ever so slightly on his heels. 'If people can't trust us then we might as well all go home now. This is a disciplinary matter. If you hadn't the wit to think about the damage you could do to Chris Chinley — or Jeremy Gleason for that matter — you could at least have thought of what it might do to you. Didn't you consider what it might mean? Kicked out or demoted. After all the years you've put in. The work you've done. Good work.'

Butchers gripped his hands tighter; his face was set and gloomy. She saw any hope die in his eyes. She paused, deliberately letting him think the worst. Then she spoke quietly. 'You don't know how lucky you are. Chris Chinley is clear on the gun residue test, his clothes are fine.'

His shoulders fell, his clenched hands slackened, his eyes shot up to scan her face then away again.

'I'll have to note an error of judgement in your records. You'll keep your stripes. Pull another stunt like this, ever,' she stressed the word, 'and you'll be suspended.'

'Thank you, boss. I know it was wrong, whatever my reasons. I just . . . thanks.' He nodded to express his gratitude, his face suffused with pink.

Richard knocked at her door and opened it, took the situation in with a glance. Looked at her questioningly — bad time? She beckoned him in.

'We're getting calls about Stone,' Richard said. 'Several from round Warrington way. We've asked the local force to give it their special attention.'

'In those spare moments they've got,' Janine remarked wryly. It was no secret that forces were stretched to the limit and under-resourced. Many areas of police work got only perfunctory attention. The relentless demand of reaching targets tended to settle priorities.

'Plus forensics on Gleason,' he held the reports in his hand. She came to stand beside him so they could scan them together. Butchers waited, all ears.

'Bloody hell,' said Janine. 'Here. Blue marking on his knees, it matches the traces found on Rosa Milicz.' She read aloud, 'Chemical analysis indicates industrial dye.'

'Blue dye works,' Butchers said in a rush, 'Heaton Mersey! It's closed down now. Kids used to play in the water there, come out blue. They pumped the effluent into the river, the mud; the banks were thick with it.' His liking for trivia coming up trumps now.

Janine felt the skin on her arms tighten and her stomach muscles contract. Another break. 'Canal?' she asked him. It might not be the place.

'River.'

Janine gestured to the map on the wall, glanced at Butchers. He moved over, pointed out the location to her. It looked good. 'Get SOCOs to meet us there,' she instructed him. 'It could be where Rosa was murdered.'

* * *

Janine rang Connie on the way, knowing that it would be impossible to get home on time. Things were happening so fast, there was so much to do. The sheer amount of work gave her a panicky feeling in her stomach, like rodents skittering about. Stupid to think about it like that. Break it down, she admonished herself, manageable chunks, one bit at a time.

Connie insisted that if Janine was going to be any later than half-seven she ring and tell her.

'Yes, and I'll get Pete over,' she replied.

'You'll let me know by ten past seven?'

'Yes. Ten past.' Janine rolled her eyes. 'Synchronise watches,' she muttered as an aside. 'Bye.' Janine turned to Richard at the wheel. 'It's like my mother's moved in — except my mother was never this organised.'

'Do the kids like her?'

'Tom does, Eleanor reckons she's bossy. Michael keeps out of her way. I think she frightens Pete — all that efficiency.'

'How is Pete?'

'OK.'

'Round yours a lot?'

She frowned. What did it matter to him? Was he jealous or something? 'It's called parenting,' she said sardonically.

'Ah.'

She thought about calling him on it but was distracted as they passed Tom's school. The crossing was festooned with mementoes for Ann-Marie: flowers in cellophane, soft toys, cards. It brought it home anew. The little girl dead, one of the men who knocked her down dead himself, the other on the run. Thankfully Chris Chinley was in the clear; she would make a point of letting him know personally. It wouldn't change the fact that she'd had to interview him while he was still mourning his loss. He'd probably never forgive her for that. She'd have to live with it. Nothing compared to what the Chinleys had to live with — or without. She looked at Richard; he pulled his mouth down, gave a little sigh. He didn't need to say anything.

* * *

The battered prefabricated building and derelict remains of stone walls were set close by the river. There was a loading area with a sheer drop into the water and it was along here that they could see the deep blue colour that had tainted both Rosa and Gleason. Originally it would have been a site for filling and unloading barges, the barrels of dye taken along the river to the canal network and then to places like Bolton and Bradford where it would be used to dye cotton and wool.

The river was a muddy brown; across the other side wire netting framed what looked like a storage depot. Orange and blue containers stacked up. A clutch of misshapen saplings sprouted at the base of the bank, bent by the force of the current. Shredded plastic bags fluttered from the branches. An urban installation.

Janine knelt beside Richard at the very edge of the stone platform. It was discoloured a rich indigo shade. Little flag markers surrounded them; scene of crime officers had already picked over this area, removing samples for testing.

'He kneels here to shove her in,' Richard was talking about Gleason. 'He gets dye on his jeans.'

'On Rosa the staining was on one side, her ankle, knee and hip. Abrasions.' Janine imagined the scene. 'If she was wrapped in bin liners and they'd torn on this edge that would account for it. The dye would get into the grazes, mark her skin.'

The wind was whipping over the water, rustling the stalks of weeds along the banks and toying with the litter here and there. Overhead, clouds with bruised edges were buffeted along. The temperature was dropping.

She looked around. 'But no sign of a struggle, nothing that fits with the state of her face. It looks like she was brought here, not killed here.'

Richard gestured behind them to the old building. 'Let's have a look in the shed.'

'Tyre prints,' one of the technicians told them. She was photographing the marks. 'One set's clearly recent. We should be able to get you a make, maybe a match.'

'I know what my money's on.' Janine hunched her shoulders up. It was cold by the riverside and even colder in the dingy warehouse. 'The Merc.'

As they walked back to his car Richard spoke. 'So supposing Stone kills her. What's his motive?'

'Maybe she won't have sex with him?'

'Bit of an overreaction.'

'Andrea said she could stand up for herself. Maybe he tries it on, rapes her even, but Rosa threatens to report him. We've no way of knowing if the sex was consensual. He realises she is serious. He has to stop her so he strangles her,' Janine suggested.

'Or Gleason. We know Gleason was here. He could have killed her?'

'Not got the same reputation, though. I can't see Gleason doing it. Let's stick with Stone. But he ropes Gleason in to help him get rid of the evidence.'

'Yes. Ditch the body, torch the car. But then the hit and run blows the thing wide open.'

Janine stopped, put a hand up to stop her hair blowing in her eyes. 'We know the car was nicked Monday night, why didn't they dump it sooner?'

'Enjoying the ride?'

'Could be — or maybe it was the other way around. What if they took the car, planning to flog it? As long as Harper never twigged they could clear what, ten, twelve grand?'

Richard nodded.

'Then while they've got it, later that night, early morning, Rosa comes into the picture. Stone tries it on, she tells him where to go, he throttles her. They bring her here, get rid. Sometime after that they hit Ann-Marie.'

'Then we pull them in but they walk, vanish as soon as they get a chance,' Richard said.

'And things go sour between them. Stone kills Gleason. Gleason knows far too much. Stone can't trust him to keep quiet; Gleason's a bag of nerves, a walking time bomb.'

'So Stone spins him some story, takes him to the tunnel and shoots him.'

They reached Richard's car. Janine looked back to the riverside, narrowing her eyes against the cold wind. 'If the tyre prints match we need to see if forensics have got anything for us from the car.'

* * *

She got the news by five that afternoon. Blood in the boot. She'd expected it but the confirmation made her back crawl. Now they just needed to see if it was Rosa's.

CHAPTER THIRTEEN

When Marta had told the others that Rosa was dead, that she'd been murdered, Zofia crossed herself and Petra swore.

'I knew it was something awful,' Petra announced.

'But why,' Zofia asked, horror vivid in her eyes, 'why would anyone do that?'

'She wanted to leave,' Marta said.

'But who . . .' Zofia was never very bright.

'Someone stopped her.'

'You think the boss . . . ?' Petra caught on.

Marta raise her eyebrows a fraction. 'It makes most sense to me.'

'The bastard, the lousy prick.'

'What are we going to do?' Zofia looked nervously at them.

'What can we do? Nothing. Keep our traps shut and carry on.' Inside, Marta felt sick with fear.

'There must be something . . .' Zofia carried on.

'And end up like she did?' Marta shouted.

Zofia shrank back, her eyes filling. She was only seventeen and emotionally even younger. A soft egg, as her babka would say. The men liked that, the schoolgirl looks, the naivety. The sadists liked her best of all, her cries were so real, her pleas rang so true.

Marta put her arm around her, pulled her close.

'I want my mama,' the girl wailed. The sentiment was so direct and unexpected that Marta felt her own eyes sting with emotion, a sudden ache inside and the memory of flinging herself into her mother's arms.

A flash of rage scorched through her. It was so unfair. Was it so wrong to want a better life? Clothes that looked halfway decent, a home and a telly, something to play music on, food in the fridge? They were all working, not thieving, working bloody hard, opening their legs for men who'd spit at them as soon as smile.

'Shush,' she told Zofia. 'It'll be OK.' It had to be and that was that.

* * *

Chris Chinley was less than appreciative of Janine's courtesy call. His hostility clear in every gesture, each word. He had opened the door a few inches — just enough to allow conversation. Janine noticed the reek of alcohol, his bloodshot eyes.

'What do you want?'

'I thought you'd like to know. The tests are clear.'

'I'm supposed to be grateful, am I?'

She tried to explain. 'Chris, you didn't give me any option. What was I supposed to do?'

He turned and walked away, leaving the door ajar and Janine on the doorstep, feeling like a right idiot.

Debbie came out.

'It's all OK.' Janine told her. 'The tests.'

'Would you like some tea?'

Janine was embarrassed by the kindness. 'I best get back.'

Horrified, she watched Debbie's face crumple. 'Janine, Chris . . . this . . . we're not going to make it.'

Janine stepped into the house, ushering Debbie with her.

'Everything's gone. Everything.' She began to cry.

Janine put her arm around her, blinking hard, breathing through her nose, tricks to control her own responses. To stop her from joining in.

* * *

Janine could smell food when she walked in home and her mouth began to water. When had she last eaten? Pete was testing Eleanor on her German, the two of them obviously having fun with it. Michael was getting a pizza out of the oven. No sign of Charlotte which meant Pete had managed to get her down. Hallelujah!

Scattering hellos and shucking off her coat she watched Tom. He was sitting alone at the table, an empty chair pulled up close to his and on the table he had laid out two lots of pens and paper and beside each a cup of milk and a saucer with slices of apple.

'Something smells good,' she said to Michael.

'Ham and pineapple.'

'You going to eat all that?'

'I was till you got here.'

'Go on,' she chided him, 'cut us a slice. You should be in bed,' she told Tom, gently.

'He's been twice,' Pete looked at her. 'And . . . er . . . Frank is back.' He jerked his head at the empty chair.

Oh, brilliant, Janine thought, suddenly understanding the duplicate snacks. That's all we need. It had been years since Tom's imaginary friend had disappeared. She was surprised he could even remember Frank well enough to recreate him.

'I wonder why,' she murmured to Pete. It was a rhetorical question.

Once the kids were all sorted she collapsed on the sofa. Her neck was stiff, she was still hungry — the pizza had barely dulled her appetite — she felt gritty and grimy from the day at work and bone tired. Had she the energy to run a bath? Would a shower do the trick? Pete was gathering his things together.

'He's not mentioned Ann-Marie today. When you told him — what did he say?'

Janine kept her face straight. 'Could he have his next party at Laser Quest?'

Pete laughed and she joined in. Kids.

'Charlotte's started the bubble thing,' Pete demonstrated, blowing a raspberry. 'I'd forgotten that bit.'

Janine gave a gasp.

'What?' Pete said.

'She's due at the clinic tomorrow — her check — I meant to ring today. I'll do it first thing. Though it wouldn't matter if we missed it, she's coming on fine — just needs to distinguish day from night.'

'Connie could take her.'

Janine wrinkled her nose. 'I'd rather go myself. I'll rearrange.'

'I think she's getting more like Michael.'

'What, moody and hormonal?'

Pete grinned. 'He spoke today. A whole sentence.'

'Can I have some money?'

'No,' he paused for effect, 'I need some new trainers.' He raised his eyebrows. 'I'll sort him out,' he added.

She began to yawn. 'I'm ready for bed.' She glanced up. Pete was watching her. She sensed a shift in the atmosphere before he even spoke.

'Janine . . . I've been thinking . . . I seem to be here most of the time as it is . . . and things . . . I know after everything that happened . . .'

She felt her pulse quicken with adrenalin. Had the urge to run away — the flight or fight syndrome.

'. . . well, you probably don't, won't . . . but when all's said and done, eighteen years . . . and I still.'

She stood, raising her palms to stop him talking. 'Don't you think it's a bit late?' She could feel the heat in her cheeks, her mouth dry. Part of her still hurt, was still hurting. He had left her, broken their marriage, walked out on his children. How could he imagine that he could reverse all that?

He cleared his throat. 'Since we had Charlotte — I was here for the others . . . the nights, everything. And it's not just missing them . . . there's you.'

'And Tina,' she said quietly.

'Maybe I was wrong.'

She was angry with him, wanted to push him, shout, break things. She ran her hand though her hair, turned away, then back. 'I can't cope with this now.'

He gave a brief nod and backed away, buttoning up his coat. She folded her arms, waited until she heard the front door close after him. Then swore softly, several times.

* * *

Chris sat in the dark in the back room. He hadn't bothered drawing the curtains; he saw the rain lash against the glass and heard the occasional whoop of police cars.

Debbie had been relieved that he was an innocent man. Some cold, cruel part of him was amused. She understood so little.

He hadn't been able to protect his daughter while she was alive and now she'd been taken from them he couldn't even avenge her death. All he had was failure. While Debbie was striving for some all-forgiving bloody Christian sainthood — Ann-Marie the martyr to her cause — he felt only fury and loathing. He couldn't read the cards that kept coming, couldn't bear the hushed condolences of people who called at the house. All wallowing in some orgy of sadness. Sad, sad, so sad. It wasn't sad — it was a fucking outrage. He still hadn't cried. He didn't want to weep and choose bouquets, he wanted to get hold of those who had killed her and beat them to a pulp. Break their faces and their teeth and burst their inner organs. But he'd had his chance and he had wavered and thought of a dozen reasons why not when there was only really one good reason — because he wasn't man enough.

Breadwinner, yes. Was that all he amounted to? If he'd known that she'd be taken so young . . . he could have made more time. Debbie had been the main one to stay home. She hadn't gone back to nursing full-time but once Ann-Marie was sleeping through she'd signed on the bank, taking one or two shifts a week to cover for sickness or holidays or the ongoing shortages. They probably could have managed without, especially as Chris's business was going well. He had work booked in up to six months ahead plus emergency work now and then. And he could name his own price. They had enough for holidays abroad, nowhere that exotic but Crete or Cyprus or, one year, Madeira. Last summer, when Ann-Marie was six they'd splashed out and gone to Disneyworld in Florida.

When Ann-Marie started school Debbie had got a part-time job at Christie's, the cancer hospital, but the school holidays were a problem. Chris could look after her but it was a bit of a daft set-up when he was making three or four times as much a day as Debbie. In the end, she went back on the bank. 'I have to do something Chris, I can't just vegetate.' And she did voluntary stuff at school too. Came home and told him stories of how this child was really struggling or the disasters that had befallen patients on the ward and the implication was always clear; we are so lucky.

And now, all over the area, families would be talking about them, the Chinleys — terrible tragedy, did you hear, the poor parents, how do you deal with something like that?

CHAPTER FOURTEEN

'Mum?' Janine was switching things off downstairs when Eleanor came down sounding worried.

'What?'

'It's Friday tomorrow.'

Janine groaned, 'Domestic science.'

'Food technology,' Eleanor corrected her impatiently.

'It's a bit late now, Ellie. What are you making?'

'Pineapple upside down cake . . .'

Yummy, thought Janine.

'I've got the ingredients,' she said. 'Connie got them for me but my apron's got all gunk on. I forgot.'

'Gunk?'

'I can't wear it like that.'

'Take another.'

'No!' Anguished. 'I want the right one.' Desperate to fit in, not to get laughed at. And when Janine thought about the aprons in the house, jokey cartoons on them, she could see her point.

Janine sighed. 'If I hand wash it now . . .'

'Can you? Oh, thank you, Mum. You're so kind.' Eleanor effused.

'Bring it here — and remember next time.'

'I will, I promise.'

After she had washed and rinsed and wrung the apron out, she placed it over one of the central heating radiators in the hall to dry

Upstairs she looked in on Tom who was fast asleep and said goodnight to Michael who was still up, playing on his PS2. 'Mum, I need some trainers.'

'Your dad said. He can take you at the weekend.' She looked at him: wrists and ankles sticking out of the chill-out suit he wore to sleep in. 'You're growing out of those,' she told him, 'you'd better get some new ones — in a bigger size — while you're in town, and anything else that doesn't fit. You're going to be enormous.'

He grinned, ducked his head with pleasure. It was such a funny age, she thought, boyish one minute and struggling to be treated as an adult the next.

In her own room, she sorted out her clothes for the following day, not bothering about noise. If Charlotte woke now and had a feed then she might go through till morning. But the infant slumbered steadily on.

Janine's mind was weaving around work: imagining Stone firing at his friend, Rosa bundled into the car boot, hearing Debbie Chinley weeping, wondering about Butchers' brother. What age had he been? And was Butchers younger or older? Had Butchers witnessed the accident? She heard the front door, Connie coming in. Janine got into her bed, sighing in appreciation at the prospect of sleep. She turned off the light and drifted off within minutes. When Charlotte woke in the night, only the once thank God, Janine got up on auto-pilot, her limbs heavy her head thick with sleep. The baby went back down without much fuss and Janine crawled back to bed.

* * *

As she opened her eyes to first light the next morning, Janine felt a skinny arm brush against hers. Tom had joined her during the night. Now he smiled at her, his eyes alert. She leant over to kiss him and he squealed. 'Watch out, you'll squash Frank.'

Oh, for pity's sake. 'Tell him to shove over, then.'

'Frank can fly,' Tom said seriously. 'He's like me, 'cept he can fly.'

Janine grunted.

'You know in heaven,' Tom said, 'do you stay with your family?'

'Yeah.'

'So, would Dad be with us?'

'Yeah.'

'What if you had two Dads?'

'I'm not sure.'

'And Tina? Would she go with us?'

Relentless logic. Janine had had enough of this conversation. 'I think the idea of heaven is that everybody's happy and everybody gets on.'

Tom turned to her, his face suddenly taut with anxiety, his eyes huge. 'Mummy, I don't want to die.'

She felt her heart clutch and she reached out to hug him. 'Oh, darling, nobody wants to die. You won't die for a long, long, long time.'

'How do you know?' he demanded. He didn't mention Ann-Marie, didn't need to.

'I just do,' she insisted. 'Nearly everybody lives to be older than Grandma and Grandpa. And you will. And heaven will have all your favourite things in and all the people you like.'

'And Frank?'

'And Frank,' she agreed.

Butchers caught her before she left home to tell her that they had confirmation on the blood from the boot of the car. It was Rosa's.

Finding each piece of the puzzle brought mixed feelings for Janine: the thrill of success, of making headway and the more melancholy acceptance of what it betrayed of the victim's last hours.

The relatively small amount of blood indicated that Rosa had already been dead when she had been placed there — her heart no longer pumping. Janine mentally ticked off what they knew so far: Rosa Milicz's battered corpse had been carried in the boot of the stolen car, she had been put in the river at the dye works, Gleason had been there and most likely Stone. The men had stolen the car from Harper, Stone's boss, and later they had accidentally killed Ann-Marie. After being questioned and released, someone, in all probability Stone, had shot Gleason. There was still a long way to go but they were moving in the right direction.

She rang Richard and shared the news. 'I've postponed the briefing. I'm going to pay a call on Harper,' she told him. 'He must have known Rosa was here illegally. I want to see what he has to say for himself. Do you want to meet me there?'

'Will do.'

* * *

Harper was still in his dressing gown when he let them in, his hair damp from the shower.

'Your car, Mr Harper, we've run some further tests. We've found traces of blood in the boot.'

He blanched at the news and looked from one to another. 'Blood? Oh, God. Are you sure?'

Janine nodded. 'We've matched it — it's Rosa's.'

'Oh, God.' He paused. 'That's horrible.'

'I don't like it either,' she said coldly.

Harper looked wary. With one hand he clasped the collar of his robe.

'Your car is stolen by your bouncer, it's used to transport the dead body of a dancer from your club . . . just exactly what is it you are not telling us?'

'Nothing.' His outrage was plausible.

'You haven't got a clue?' Richard asked him.

'No, honestly, I . . .'

'Not an inkling?'

'No.'

'I don't buy it,' Janine said sharply.

He met her gaze, the eyelid on his lazy eye flickering for a moment. He gave a little snort.

'Rosa was here illegally,' she pressed on.

'I didn't know that.'

'No?'

'No. I'd never have taken her on.'

'Really? I got the impression that you weren't all that bothered about record keeping, documents and the like.'

'That's different — something like this, we could get closed down, couldn't we?'

'When did you last see Rosa?'

'We've been over all this,' he exploded. 'Why can't you people just accept that I don't know anything about it. I'm sorry she's dead but I've no idea who killed her. I'd no idea she was illegal. End of story.'

'You didn't answer my question, Mr Harper,' Janine said flatly, 'when did you last see her?'

He pivoted away and back, sighing. He pinched the bridge of his thin nose as if garnering patience. 'Sunday, at work.' He dropped his hand and made eye contact with her, trying to stare her out. She looked away first, deliberately — not prepared to play his little game. 'We'll need to talk to you again,' she said, 'I'm sure.'

As he showed them out he spoke to Richard. 'I was thinking, the car insurance, will I have to explain all this?'

Richard gave a harsh laugh. Janine glared at him. Was the man for real? Neither of them dignified his query with an answer.

Outside, Richard said, 'Bring him in to get him talking?'

'On what grounds? We've verified the taxi, the casino, the report of the stolen car.' She sighed. The fact that Stone had taken Harper's car still niggled her — it seemed so reckless. Why take that one rather than a stranger's? Fouling his own backyard.

'What if Harper was mixed up in it and Rosa was killed before his car got nicked?' Richard suggested.

She swivelled her eyes, 'Then why report the car stolen, why not keep schtum?'

'OK, scotch that. Besides,' he admitted, 'we can tie Gleason and Stone to the car and to the dumping of the body.'

'We'll run background checks on Harper — see if that throws up anything. I trust my instincts . . .' She opened the passenger door.

Richard raised his eyebrows, waiting for more.

'. . . and my instincts say he's involved.' She settled back into the seat. She looked at Richard as he got behind the wheel. 'All we need to do is find out how.'

'Piece of cake,' he laughed.

'Well, it might not be easy,' she granted, 'but all things are possible and we're not going to let Mr Harper so much as draw a breath without looking into it.'

* * *

Lee Stone's known family (ex-foster mother, two sisters and a half-brother) had been visited — none of them had seen or heard from him.

'No, love. He never kept in touch,' said his foster mother. 'Shock seeing him on the telly like that. And you reckon he shot this other bloke?'

'Haven't seen him for years,' his half-brother said when the officers talked to him in the pub he ran. 'We're not exactly close. In fact the last time I saw him he tried to flog us a dodgy motor. I told him I wasn't interested. And I'm still not.'

'If he does get in touch you'll let us know?'

'My pleasure.'

'Might do.' Stone's younger sister offered when asked the same question at the launderette where she worked. 'Would there be any money in it? A reward like?' She was twenty and heavily overweight, her eyes darkened with kohl, her hair straw-like, high gloss on her lips. Her tongue worried at a cold sore at the corner of her mouth.

'Not at this stage.'

She grunted. 'He's a bit handy with his fists, our Lee. I wouldn't want to make an enemy of him. If he knew I'd put you onto him . . .' She shuddered.

'We wouldn't divulge any names.'

'He might guess though. I know it's not right if he's owt to do with that shooting . . .' she wrinkled her nose, shrugged, 'but it might never happen.'

The elder sister, contacted at a call centre in Hyde, was more succinct. 'Fuck off, he's my brother, and I'm no grass.'

Discreet enquiries were made at The King's Head and The Willows as well as the Pool Hall on the main road. No one had seen hide nor hair of the man. And no one had a good word to say about him.

CHAPTER FIFTEEN

Butchers took an hour, an early lunch. He drove down through Rusholme, stopped on the curry mile for a beef biryani take-away and ate it in the car. From there he made his way through Withington and west towards Chorlton.

It was years since he'd been down here. He parked on a side road and walked up to the gates, feeling a lurch of anxiety: the place looked different and he couldn't remember which way to go. After a while he got his bearings, walking through the huge, flamboyant graves with their biers and angels and elaborate carvings to the more modern sections behind.

He found the place. The lettering on the grey, mottled marble had originally been painted in gold. A lot of it had faded though the carved dedication still ran clear.

ANDREW COLIN BUTCHERS
1 MAY 1974 — 22 JUNE 1983
BELOVED SON AND BROTHER
REST IN PEACE

He gave a heavy sigh, felt the old sensation of grief lodge in his chest. Never done with it. He had been fifteen when Andy had gone, Andy just nine. He had been drenched in guilt and impotent rage. Why hadn't he been kinder to his brother, why had it been him and not Ian? The last memory he had was lodged like a splinter in his heart; telling Andy not to touch his tapes again or he'd bloody batter him, the flash of resentment on the lad's face. And Ian had driven himself half mad with blame. If he hadn't yelled at Andy he might have gone out to play later. Five minutes — it would have saved him. Ian had worked away at the guilt, poking at the wound, helping it to fester and sting.

He had never said anything to his parents. Couldn't. They had folded, collapsing in on themselves, behaving like zombies: blank, empty, hollowed out.

As that first Christmas had approached he'd found himself drowning. He barely slept, he stayed off school. He had stomach-ache and terrible migraines. There was no point to anything anymore.

One afternoon he bought a bottle of rum at the corner shop. He took it up into the little wood near the railway cutting. The trains went through every half hour. He drank the rum in big gulps, burning him as it went down.

It was cold and the light was fading as he finished the bottle. He checked his watch and scrambled clumsily down the bank. It was thick with brambles which cut painful gouges in his legs and his hands and arms.

He stood at the side of the tracks, feet unsteady on the large lumps of gravel. It was nearly dark and there was no lighting along this section of the track.

He strained to hear the train coming but the rails and the overhead wires were silent. He caught the sound of scrabbling from the bank opposite. Some creature moving about: cat or squirrel or hedgehog.

He waited but no train came. He couldn't see to read his watch anymore. His eyes felt hot and his head spun. He felt the sudden clench in his guts, a wash of saliva flood his mouth and then the rush of vomit. He doubled over and was sick all over his shoes. Over and over until there was just a sour, watery foam.

Left with a raging thirst and a devastating headache he climbed back up the bank, lashing back at the thorns that lacerated him.

When he stumbled into the house, reeking and bleeding and insolent his mother flew at him. Her harsh words were the first sign of passion since Andy's death.

His father, arriving back from work and told of his behaviour, had instructed him to pull himself together, sort himself out and get a bloody job if he was done with school. He then made Ian clean his own shoes and put his clothes in the washing machine.

After he had had a bath his mother had wiped the gashes on his limbs with TCP. It had been agony.

He applied for the police force the following week. Not with any noble intention: it was a job, and they said you got accommodation at a good rate too.

He wondered if his parents still came here, on Andy's birthday perhaps. Or more often? He had no idea. He couldn't remember the last time any of them had spoken of Andy. Their way of coping perhaps.

The name was unfamiliar now, making a strange shape in the mouth. Saying it aloud would be shocking, sharp and hurtful. A gust of wind tore through the cemetery, tugging trees low and sending leaves and vases and flowers rolling over the bright turf. Butchers shivered. Time to go.

'See you, our kid.' He felt a bit of a prat speaking aloud. The wind made his eyes water. He gave a good sniff and set off for his car.

* * *

Rosa had not needed a pregnancy test. As soon as she stood upright in the morning she would start retching. She admitted to Marta that her breasts were tender and she felt exhausted — they knew it wasn't an illness. It had happened to one of the girls before; they reckoned she had been pregnant before she left Poland. It was fixed for her to go to a clinic, a private arrangement with no documents required. The fee, a thousand pounds sterling, had been added to her resettlement debt and she was back at work within the week. The same doctor came every thirteen weeks to give them the jabs. That was meant to stop any babies and it got rid of periods too so they could work all month, every month without any problems. When Rosa had become really down and also started to gain weight they let her skip the jab. She moved to the club then so she didn't have to stay on the drug.

'They won't let you keep it,' Marta told her.

Rosa was sitting on her bed, her arms around her stomach, her face paler than usual. She stared at Marta. 'I can't do that,' Rosa said.

Marta folded her arms. You might not have any choice, she thought.

'No,' Rosa said, her mouth set hard. 'No.' Flint in her eyes.

Marta left it a day or two, waiting to find a good time to talk again. But it was Rosa who had spoken first, as she spread margarine on toast, her back to her friend who sat at the kitchen table. 'I'm going to keep the baby, Marta. I'm going to go home.'

'You can't! You still owe money.'

'I don't care.'

Marta had stood up, gone round beside her, and touched her shoulder, forcing her to look. 'Rosa, see sense. They won't let you. And what would you be going back to, stinking nappies in that crowded flat? What sort of life is that?'

'It's my baby.'

'They'll never let you go, Rosa. Don't be stupid. Don't even think about it.'

Tears had sprung in Rosa's eyes and she had caught the side of her lip between her teeth. She had pushed away from the counter angrily and walked out, leaving her toast uneaten.

* * *

Shap was having another go at Andrea. He had enough experience of joints like Topcat to know there was always the chance of something a little more intimate if you asked in the right quarters. And he reckoned if Rosa had been doing more than dancing they needed to find out who she had been playing out with.

Andrea was doing her make-up in the cramped room that served as a changing area for the girls.

'What if a punter wants something extra?'

'Won't get it here,' she said flatly.

'Come on, Andrea. You've got someone hassling you, he wants the full English . . . French . . . Polish?'

'I dance, that's all.'

Shap was getting brassed off with this. 'And the other girls? Some of them would want the extra cash.' He watched her apply lip-liner. 'Did Rosa ever make special arrangements?'

'I don't know, I don't think so.'

'What if someone won't take no for an answer?'

'Like you?' she snapped.

He sighed. He wasn't convinced by her; he'd keep digging, talking to people round the place and have another go at Andrea later. Turned out it happened sooner rather than later.

He struck lucky with a drunk he met in the urinals. One of those blokes who get all mushy and genial after a few whisky chasers. Shap was trying the indirect approach. Playing up as one of the lads, having a grumble about the petty rules they had at places like this. 'Honest,' he told the soak, 'place in town, my mate gives her a little squeeze and next thing they sling us all out. Sometimes you want more than just a look, don't you?'

'You tried the other place, in Openshaw? Anything you want there.'

Shap's eyes lit up. 'A club?'

'Knocking shop. Nice girls, straight off the plane. Eager to please.'

'I might just do that,' Shap told him. 'Thanks, mate. You take it easy now.'

Shap stuck his head round the door of the dressing room. She was fiddling with her hair, tweaking the ends as he came in.

'Openshaw. Ring any bells?'

He saw her eyes flicker but she recovered quickly. She kept her mouth shut.

'We're not interested in soliciting or living on immoral earnings, Andrea. Rosa's murder — that's why we're asking.' He watched her, could see her hesitate. He kept waiting, reckoning that another push might mess it up. Then she grabbed her bag, the bracelets on her arm clinking together. She rummaged inside it then handed him a small business card. Just a logo on it; a couple of pen strokes suggesting a reclining woman, and a phone number. 'I never gave you it.'

'You ever work there?'

Andrea shook her head.

'What about Rosa?'

She pressed her lips together, crossed her arms, looked away from him for a minute then back. Uneasy. Finally she gave a nod.

* * *

It was the break they'd been hoping for. When Shap rang and told her, Janine felt like kissing the phone. She instructed him to return to the station.

'It's all very hush-hush,' Shap said, when the team met in the incident room.

'Any bog-standard massage parlour they'd have an ad in the papers, number in the phone book.' Richard agreed.

'You think they're illegals?' Janine asked him.

'Yes, like Rosa.'

'The Polish connection,' she mused. She called over one of the DCs and told him to get more on Sulikov, the owner of the Topcat Club and, in all likelihood, the Openshaw brothel. 'See what Poland can give us, any criminal record, current activities and so on.'

She turned back to Shap. 'Well — what are we waiting for?'

He held out the card Andrea had given him. 'The address.'

'Ah.' She smiled. 'You can be our Trojan Horse, Shap.'

'Donkey,' Richard corrected her. 'New customer. After the full monty.'

Shap pulled out his mobile phone and began to dial. Then, to Janine's surprise and amusement, spots of colour bloomed on his face. 'Can I have a bit of privacy, or what?' he said belligerently.

Shap shy. Who'd have thought it.

CHAPTER SIXTEEN

They waited down the street, in cars, watching the house for a few minutes, getting the measure of the place. Unremarkable; it looked like any of the other large semi-detached houses. They were built of the brick so common in the city, with sloping grey slate roofs and bay windows. Each property had a garage at the end of a short driveway. Most of the gardens were neat. The one at the house had been concreted over — ultimate low maintenance, and a low brick wall replaced the iron railings or hedging of the other houses. But still there was nothing to betray its nature. Not until the door opened and a man walked briskly away, crossing the street diagonally and distancing himself from the place. Not exactly furtive but certainly fast.

'Let's go,' said Janine.

They followed Shap, but were careful to leave enough of a gap so that whoever answered the door wouldn't realise they were all together.

Shap pressed the buzzer for the intercom at the side of the front door.

'Yes?' A woman's voice answered.

'I've got an appointment,' Shap answered, 'it's Mickey.'

The buzzer blared and Shap pushed the door open. Janine and Richard moved forward quickly, following him in. Behind them a clutch of junior officers, briefed to make sure no one left the building.

The blonde woman in the hall tried to bolt, darting for the stairs, but Richard caught her arm. 'There's nowhere to go,' he told her. 'Let's just sit down and have a talk.'

While others searched the place, Janine and Richard went into a downstairs room which obviously served as a waiting area. The room was overheated and stuffy. It smelt of cigarette smoke, industrial strength perfume and gloss paint from the central heating radiator. A disconcerted client was escorted out to talk to Shap in the kitchen.

Janine introduced herself and Richard and they showed the woman their police ID cards.

'Can I have your name?' Richard asked her.

She hesitated a moment then seemed to resign herself to the situation. 'Marta Potocki.' Her English was heavily accented. She wore a flimsy blouse, a lacy black bra visible beneath it, a tight red mini-skirt. She was barefoot, hands and toe nails painted fire-engine red.

'Are you Polish?' Janine asked.

She nodded.

'Marta, did you know Rosa Milicz?'

The woman closed her eyes for a moment, she swallowed and gave a jerky nod. 'And you know Rosa has been killed?' Janine said gently.

Marta nodded, biting her cheeks and compressing her lips.

'I'm sorry' Janine told her. She waited a moment. 'We're investigating her murder. Do you know anything about Rosa's death?'

Marta shook her head. 'No.'

'Did Rosa live here?'

'Yes.'

'Please can you show us her room.'

They followed Marta up the stairs and into a small, sparsely furnished room at the back. There were two small twin beds, shabby curtains, a white particleboard wardrobe and a mock beech vanity unit with a mottled mirror. Janine realised the girls slept here but would entertain clients in one of the other larger and presumably more comfortably furnished bedrooms.

Nothing to suggest that the murder had happened here, no blood splashes or missing carpets. But Rosa had been strangled — she might have been killed in one place, leaving little evidence behind, then moved somewhere else for the messy mutilation. They would have this place examined anyway.

There were few personal possessions: make-up and hair dressing items on the unit, an old magazine, a tatty pocket dictionary.

'How long had Rosa lived here?'

'About six months,' Marta rubbed at her upper arms.

'And was she working here?'

'In the beginning. Then just the dancing.'

Janine looked round the room again, imagined the girl dividing her time between the Topcat Club and this place. No life of glamour. She moved to look out of the window. It overlooked the flat roof of an extension at the back and an unkempt patch of garden, a row of houses beyond.

'When did you last see Rosa?' Richard asked.

'Monday. She went out about four.'

'Where?'

'She said she was going to work.'

'She never showed up.'

Janine picked up the dictionary.

'She thought maybe one day, to teach,' Marta said, then bit her lip.

'We'd like to talk to everyone who works here — down in the front room,' Janine said.

* * *

There were just three of them, dressed similarly in sheer tops and short skirts. The youngest looking, who gave her name as Zofia, had a pair of pink, fluffy mules on her feet, the sort of thing Eleanor would wear. Petra wore shoddy gold sandals. Shap stood by the door, Richard near the window while Janine took one of the red velvet chairs that the girls were also sitting on. Janine established that they were all Polish and had no official papers. She explained why the police were there and that they would be asking them some initial questions about Rosa. After that they would be taking them to the police station where they would be interviewed by immigration authorities.

The girls were quiet and morose.

'Has there been any trouble? Anyone bothering Rosa? Perhaps someone with a score to settle?'

Marta shook her head. None of the others moved.

'Do you know this man?' She held up a photograph of Lee Stone. She saw recognition in their expressions.

'He brought us here. He drives the van,' Marta told her.

'From Poland?'

'No, here. In UK.'

'For Mr Sulikov?' The name provoked a ripple of reaction. Zofia shifted her position, crossing her arms and legs. Petra flashed Marta a warning look. Marta didn't say anything.

'Konrad Sulikov?'

No one answered. They sat unmoving except for Petra who was swinging one foot to and fro, the sandal dangling and slapping against her sole.

'Marta?' Janine said.

Marta gave a reluctant, almost imperceptible dip of the head.

There was a noise outside and Richard drew back the corner of the net curtains. 'Transport's here,' he said. 'And scene of crime are on their way.'

Marta frowned and looked at Janine.

'We're still trying to establish where Rosa was killed,' Janine explained.

'But she went out. She never came back here.'

'We have to make sure. Marta, did Rosa have a boyfriend?'

'Only Mr Harper.'

Harper! Janine felt a rush of shock.

'What?' Richard exclaimed.

'Harper?' Janine said, struggling to absorb it. 'Rosa and Harper?'

'Yeah,' Marta looked a little disconcerted at their reactions. 'He takes care of this place.'

'Harper!' Janine looked at Richard, shaking her head with incredulity, her skin tingling. 'I bloody knew there was something. I knew it.'

* * *

Once the minibus had left to take the girls to the police station, Janine, Richard and Shap clustered in the hallway.

'He's not just being economical with the truth — his story's got more holes than a string vest,' Janine said. 'He was sleeping with her for God's sake. He knew she was living at the brothel, he's running the place. The woman's dead and he doesn't say a word.'

'The pair of them kept it bloody quiet,' said Shap. 'No one at the club knew.'

'You sure about that? Not just keeping their mouths shut?' Janine asked.

'Andrea rang in,' Richard pointed out. 'If she'd known Harper was seeing Rosa, I think she would have told us.'

'She didn't tell us about this place, not till she absolutely had to.' She took in the striped wallpaper, the cheap nylon carpet, the tasselled shade on the ceiling lamp.

'Not the same though,' said Shap. 'She knew this place was off the books, maybe even knew that Harper was running it. But if Andrea had known Harper was going with Rosa and then seen him deny it when she'd been killed, she would have shopped him.'

Janine thought he was right. 'OK, so Rosa and Harper kept their affair under wraps at the club but, more to the point, why did he keep quiet about his relationship with Rosa when he spoke to us?'

''Cos she was illegal and he was up to his neck in it, managing the brothel, sex slaves near enough,' Shap pointed out.

Richard raised an eyebrow.

'They were hardly at liberty,' Janine agreed.

'Or he kept quiet because he killed her,' Richard said simply.

Shap looked from one to another, the question plain on his face.

'I don't know,' Janine answered. 'That's for us to find out, isn't it? No harm in giving him the impression we favour him for it. He's been mucking us about for long enough. Let's shake him up.'

Richard looked at her with interest.

'We'll arrest him for her murder. That should loosen his tongue. And while we're about it, you,' she said to Shap, 'can have another of your little chats with Andrea.'

* * *

There was quite a crowd at the club when they got there; Friday afternoon and men starting the weekend off early. Groups of office workers or sales reps, be-suited but already dishevelled, their jackets discarded and ties loosened or removed. The crowd looked particularly young, early twenties Janine guessed, and half-drunk. Probably not stop boozing till Sunday night. Weekends spent smashed in an attempt to escape the stress of the working week. Could be a stag night, she thought.

Andrea was dancing, though her eyes flew to them as soon as she realised they'd come in. Harper was seated at a table, playing host to a couple of customers. He made an apology to his companions and stood up to meet Janine and Richard.

'Not again,' he thrust his hands in his pockets.

Janine smiled; there was no warmth in it. 'James Harper,' she said, 'I am arresting you on suspicion of the murder of Rosa Milicz.' A wave of disquiet travelled round the club as people sensed the change in atmosphere. Andrea stopped dancing. 'You do not have to say anything. But it may harm your defence if you do not mention something which you later rely on in court. Anything you do say may be given in evidence. Is there anything you would like to say?'

'You've got it all wrong.' Harper was pallid with shock. Tremors worked in the muscles round his jaw line. He spread his arms out, palms up; look no tricks. 'I don't know anything about it.' He turned to the tables behind him as if recruiting them to his side, 'This is complete lunacy.'

* * *

Shap followed Andrea through to the changing room. She looked shaken. Understandable. Not a nice thought that your boss might be a murderer.

'We've been to the brothel,' he said. 'You know much about it?'

'Nothing,' she said flatly.

'They're all illegals — girls from Poland.'

She bit at her lip, looking anxious.

Shap slid his backside onto the corner of one of the tables. 'Andrea, you told us Rosa didn't have a boyfriend.'

'She didn't.' She looked confused. 'Not that she told me about anyway.'

'What if I told you Harper and Rosa had a thing going on?'

She gave a sharp laugh, humourless. 'They didn't.'

Shap nodded slowly. He saw the disbelief alter Andrea's face. She blinked a couple of times, laughed again. 'Honestly? You really think he . . .'

'We don't know yet but we have our suspicions.'

'The bastard,' she whispered. 'How could he do that?'

'Allegedly,' Shap said. He offered her a cigarette, lit one himself.

She sighed.

'That surprise you?'

'I thought he was an OK bloke, you know? Fair. Turns out . . .'

'. . . he's just like the rest of us?'

She glared at him, her eyes fierce.

'We're not all the same,' he said. He studied her for a moment, took a pull on his cigarette. 'What about you?' he tried to sound casual. 'You seeing anyone?' He smiled.

'Only my husband,' she retorted.

Shap's face fell. He liked Andrea, young and pretty, with a bit of a gob on her — but husbands he could do without.

Shelley bustled into the room, peeling off a tight, white leather jacket. 'What's going on?'

'They've arrested Jimmy.'

'What for?'

'Rosa.'

''Kin 'ell.' Shelley stared at Shap. 'That right?'

He nodded.

'God!' she exclaimed. 'That is really creepy. That's horrible, that is. What about this place? What'll happen?'

'We haven't charged him,' Shap told her.

'But you've taken him in,' Andrea said.

'Just think, could have been any of us,' Shelley said dramatically to Andrea. 'Working with him, day in day out. Turns my stomach. That poor girl.'

'Don't hang your boots up just yet,' Shap said crossing over to the door. 'Innocent until proven guilty.'

The looks they gave him, full on and cynical, said it all.

'Yeah,' Andrea folded her arms, 'you're just saying that in case you can't pin it on him.'

'You wouldn't arrest him if you hadn't something on him,' Shelley added.

Shap held up a hand. 'Happens all the time. He lied to us, we don't like that.'

'And he was sleeping with her,' Andrea told Shelley.

'He never was.'

Andrea nodded.

'They're always prime suspects,' Shelley said knowingly.

'The bastard,' Andrea said quietly and a silence settled between them.

CHAPTER SEVENTEEN

At the station, Harper immediately demanded his own solicitor. While arrangements were made, Richard and Janine caught up with other events, taking reports from officers staffing the incident room.

'All known haunts covered for Stone — no joy,' Richard summarised.

'Someone must know where he is,' Janine complained. The man's face had been plastered the length and breadth of the country 'Any more sightings in Warrington?'

They looked at the log. Nothing had been added in the last few hours. 'Did you speak to them?' she asked Richard.

'Butchers did. But maybe . . .'

They might get more cooperation from the neighbouring force if a request came from a more senior rank. Janine nodded. 'I'll call — though it looks like he's moved on going by that log.'

'Boss.' Another detective constable had brought them coffee and biscuits. Janine took a cup and chocolate bourbon; she bit into the biscuit and took a sip of the drink. Drinkable. Just. She had her own coffee maker in her office but when things got crazy like this there wasn't time to stop and make a decent brew. So much for her fond imaginings of relaxed child-free coffee breaks.

Richard was handed another folder. 'From Poland, sir,' the young DC explained.

Richard riffled through the faxes.

'Let's see.' Janine moved closer. She wondered how long Sulikov had been smuggling women. How many Rosas and Marta had left family, home, friends and country to wash up in sleazy suburban brothels at the whim of men like Harper? 'Do Poland know he's into this?' Janine asked Richard.

'No reference here, but this is all history,' he said dismissively. 'They're still collating further data.' He scanned the document. 'Started out as a teenager in gangs — smuggling alcohol and cigarettes.'

'More money in human cargo these days,' Janine observed. She was forming an image in her mind of the Pole: broad Slavic face, high forehead and wide cheekbones, a balding head, perhaps a scar. A cliché, she realised, a stereotype conjured up by the fearful reactions of the young women when his name had been mentioned, married to a clutch of corny images from Second World War films. She, of all people, should know that killers came in many guises: the bland and the attractive just as likely to be perpetrators as the wild or ugly-looking.

And a trafficker like Sulikov could rely on the silence of the people he transported. Living beyond the law, the illicit workers and their associates forfeit any protection from it. Unable to get help if they were robbed, beaten, starved or forced to work in dangerous situations. The death by drowning of nineteen Chinese cockle pickers in Morecambe Bay had sounded a wake-up call to government, but while the underlying cause of poverty and desperation remained there would always be people prepared to take a risk. And people making money from that need.

She looked at the clock. It was three-twenty. 'What's the time difference, here and Poland?'

'They're an hour ahead. I'll get someone onto it now.'

'Tell them it's urgent. We don't want to be hanging around waiting for them to get on board.'

'I'll ask them to take a look at his place. See if he's there.'

'Yes, but emphasise we don't want him tipped off. And ask them for a photo. I'm trying to fix a meeting with Immigration — see how we handle it.'

'Their way.'

'Usually.'

There was often disagreement between local teams like hers and the immigration service on how over-stayers or illegal entrants were handled. Immigration, bound up in their own numbers game, favoured speedy deportations enabling them to tick boxes, though many acknowledged that the approach severely limited attempts to gather intelligence on the bigger players behind the scenes. For detectives it could mean watching while suspects or victims of other crimes were bundled away leaving a case in tatters.

'Is The Lemon in?'

Richard nodded and she went to see if her boss could be of any help.

* * *

'I've arrested Harper on suspicion, sir,' Janine told DCS Hackett. 'I need to begin interviews with him soon as his brief arrives. He was seeing Rosa Milicz as well as managing the brothel where she lived.'

'And Stone?' Hackett's shrewd eyes scrutinised her.

'He's implicated too. He drove the van, bringing the women in. I'm hoping the women can tell me more about both men — and about Sulikov; we've still very little on him. Can we keep them here until I have a chance to talk to them, properly?'

'Sorry, I've already had Immigration on, they want them at the removal centre near Leeds as soon as possible.'

'I don't want them deported.'

He leant forward, his head tilted to one side. 'There's not much chance of that — this is a murder enquiry. I've made that quite clear. Will the girls talk?'

'Probably not — especially as we're treating them like criminals. They've been falsely imprisoned to all intents and purposes; no passports, no outdoor shoes or clothing. They signed up for dancing or waitressing, not prostitution.'

'Are we talking murder or trafficking here?' He was warning her to stick to the case.

'The two may well be linked.'

'Don't lose your focus.'

'No, sir. But I won't get much chance to find out, will I?'

'Not unless you get a move on. Though there is a road network between here and Leeds, Janine, if push comes to shove.'

Sarky git.

She got up to leave.

'And your leak?' he said sourly.

As if it was some fault in her own plumbing. 'Plugged,' she told him.

He waited.

'Ian Butchers. He was too close to the case, had a young brother killed in a hit and run.'

He gave a weary sigh, made as if to speak, hesitated. Then, 'You disregarding procedure?'

'Chris Chinley has been exonerated.'

'Nevertheless. Can you imagine . . .'

'But it didn't, sir.' She blushed as she interrupted him, aware that this was dicey ground. Never interrupt a senior officer. Hanging offence; drawing and quartering too with a boss like Hackett. But she ploughed on, 'We'd gain nothing from launching a formal disciplinary — we'd lose a decent copper with over twenty years' service.'

'I don't know that I can approve that decision.'

She felt an edge of anger that he would dismiss her arguments. And an eddy of anxiety as she prepared to tackle him. Her skin felt slightly clammy. 'I don't think you need to, sir. It's sorted.'

He glared at her, gimlet-eyed. She could tell it was touch and go but she didn't volunteer anything more. She'd had plenty of run-ins with Hackett in the past and had come to learn that he appreciated it when his officers stood their ground and confronted him head on. She felt heat crawl up her back as she waited, her mouth dry.

He gave a crisp nod of dismissal. Her legs felt weak when she got out into the corridor, as if she had been running uphill.

She found Marta in the yard, having a cigarette, waiting to be transported to the removal centre. It was cold out there; the grey sky promised rain; Janine thought she felt a spot of drizzle in the air. The miserable light signalled the end of the afternoon. Janine shivered and buttoned her coat.

'What was going on with Rosa?' Janine asked her.

Marta took a breath, began to speak, then tried again as her words caught and emotion flushed through her face. 'She wanted to go home. She was having a baby, she wanted to keep the baby. I told her; don't be stupid, they'll stop you. It's dangerous,' she spoke animatedly. 'Sometime she tells me maybe she can turn herself in to the police. Crazy. What about us, then where would we all be?' She shook her head. 'But Rosa was going home. Once she makes up her mind.' She blew air out of her lips, 'pouf.' A gesture of exasperation.

'Who killed her?' Janine asked quietly.

Marta looked away, smoked her cigarette. 'I don't know.'

'Who do you think killed her?' Janine continued to watch her, forcing her to make eye contact. When Marta finally spoke Janine had to strain to hear.

'I'm very afraid to tell you this.' She rubbed at her upper arms, turned her head from side to side as though checking for eavesdroppers. 'Very afraid.'

'Please, Marta.'

She shuddered. 'Sulikov, I think — his bully boys. Now no one else will think of trying to get away.'

Janine felt her pulse kick and quicken. Suspects, and a motive. Now they'd found the brothel, now they'd found

Marta, things were opening up. Some cases were like this; you'd batter away for days, weeks even, and then the first crack would appear. It was always a liberating moment no matter how grim the circumstances.

'What's he like, Sulikov?'

'I never met him.'

'But you knew of him in Poland?'

'Yes. He was the man, the boss. A very bad man.'

'What about Harper?' It would be useful to know what Marta thought about him before she and Richard interviewed him.

'He let her dance at the club and Rosa thought he was a prince,' she said bitterly. 'He would never go against his boss. He's not a brave man. He was using her. She loved him, he screwed her. Just like they all do,' Marta paused. 'She was thinking of names,' she said, 'of little clothes . . .' Her eyes watered, she wiped at a tear smudging her make-up. Her nose reddened. A tug of wind wrapped her blonde hair about her face.

'Could he have killed her?'

'Harper?' Marta seemed sceptical.

'When you said bully boys . . .'

'Lee Stone,' Marta suggested.

Not Harper then? What had his role been — just to keep quiet? Or had he told Sulikov Rosa was talking about leaving — had he set the wheels in motion and then walked away?

Janine watched a magpie land across the other side of the yard by the rubbish bins. It bounced a step or two and then began to stab at something on the ground. Its mate joined it. The harsh calls of the birds echoed round the concrete square. Two for joy, Janine thought. Hard to see from where she was standing. Did they have that rhyme in Poland? Did they have magpies?

'You don't know where Rosa was heading?'

'I thought she was going into work. Well, that's what she said but now, thinking of it, she was . . .' Marta struggled to find an English word, 'a little strange, like she was hiding something.' She nodded. 'She was running away.'

'Since then — have you heard anything, from Lee Stone or Harper? Have they said anything at all that might help us?'

'We've not seen them.' Marta finished her cigarette, dropped it on the floor into a convenient puddle. It died with a little hiss.

Janine thought again of the bleak room that had been Rosa's home, of the squalid life she'd led, servicing men at the brothel and then gyrating for them at the club. Putting her hopes in Harper. And it had all ended with one of the men, maybe Stone, strangling her.

The other two girls appeared, lighting up as soon as they emerged through the double doors. They both looked pale and tired.

'The girls,' Janine said, 'some of them, they must know what they're really going to end up doing. People must know it's going on.'

'Oh, you know do you? You have experience, yes?' Marta said hotly. After a moment she added in a softer tone, 'Maybe we know. But there's always a chance, something better here. Back home, nothing.' She shook her head very slowly. 'No hope. Nothing.'

CHAPTER EIGHTEEN

Harper's solicitor, a bullish looking man with a bad complexion and an excellent tailor, had arrived and sat with his client facing Janine and Richard. Harper looked anxious, a frown lodged between his eyes, his fingers tangled together on the table in front of him. A small tic fretted at the left side of his jaw.

'You've rather a lot of explaining to do,' Janine told him. 'Let's start with Rosa Milicz, shall we?'

'She danced at the club . . .' he began, sounding weary at repeating the same information.

'Don't waste your breath,' Janine interrupted him. 'We know about your relationship. We know you were her pimp.'

His expression shifted, concern replacing the jaded look. 'I . . .' he faltered. 'I liked her. We hit it off. She couldn't settle, though. Some of them, they get used to being on the game but she hated it. So I let her work at the club, instead. But she still wasn't happy.'

'She was pregnant,' Janine said.

Harper blinked. It backed up her hunch. 'It was yours,' she stated.

He looked a little uneasy. 'She said it was.'

'You thought she was lying?'

A moment then he swung his head, no. He pressed his palms against the table and ducked his head as if steeling himself. 'She began to talk about going back. She had nothing over there.' He implied her decision was ridiculous.

'Family?'

Harper shrugged. Either he didn't know what family Rosa had or he didn't think it relevant. 'I said I'd try and find a way, smooth things over. Then Sunday night, at work, she's on about it again, getting in a state. I told her maybe I could persuade Sulikov to let her go — tell him she was seriously ill or something. But I needed some time.' He spoke calmly, plenty of eye contact. 'I told her to wait. I thought I'd got through to her.' He shook his head.

Richard moved position. 'Did you see Rosa on Monday?'

'No,' Harper said. 'I told you.'

'You were close to Rosa,' said Janine, 'but maybe a baby wasn't part of the plan. Convenient for you — her disappearance.'

Harper's face fell, his mouth opened as he reacted to the implication. 'No, it wasn't like that.'

'You were sleeping with her, you were the father of her child and yet when she was murdered you said nothing.' Janine challenged him to justify his actions.

'I was scared,' he protested.

'She was dead.'

He flinched.

Janine carried on, hoping that more pressure would push him into talking. 'Tell us, Mr Harper. What really happened? You killed her, didn't you?'

'No,' a wobble of panic in his voice. 'I didn't touch her.' He looked from Janine to Richard. His eyes shone with intensity. 'I don't know what you want me to say.'

'The truth would be a start. How about something like this?' In considering Harper as the killer, Janine had already formulated an account of events that didn't stray too far from the few facts they had. 'You did see her on Monday: she told her friend that she was going into work but she came to you and you had sex. She told you she was running away. You had to stop her leaving.' Janine laid out each part of the scenario in a matter-of-fact voice. 'You argued. You put your hand around her neck. How long did it take?'

In the pause she watched Harper's Adam's apple bob up and down, a bead of sweat break on his forehead and start to trace its path down his cheek.

'And then you wrapped her in bin bags. Broke her face.'

'Her face!' He was appalled. 'I didn't kill her. I wouldn't hurt her. It wasn't me.'

'Who was it then?' Janine said sharply.

'I can't,' Harper said fervently, shaking his head quickly. 'It's not safe. He . . .'

'Who?'

The solicitor interrupted the exchange. 'My client has answered your questions.'

'He's told me nothing,' Janine retorted. 'Who was it, Mr Harper?'

'I can't,' he insisted. 'Please, I can't.' His forehead was furrowed with lines, he grimaced, his lips pulled back, spittle at the corners of his lips. 'I just can't.'

Janine made to stand, fed up with pussyfooting about. She'd call his bluff. 'Fine. If that's the way you want it. Interview terminated.'

'All right!' Harper shouted. 'All right. Sulikov, it was Sulikov. But I can't . . .' he lowered his voice. 'It was a warning.' He ran his hands over his face and breathed out harshly. 'I'm sorry I can't — he'll kill me.'

'What do you mean? A warning?' Richard asked.

Harper slid his hands down his face leaving his fingertips splayed across his jaw, his little fingers covering the deep cleft in his chin. He sounded hoarse. 'It was a warning, to the girls, to me.' He spread his hands out now, palms upwards asking to be believed. 'I don't know if he actually did it or whether he paid someone else. He rang me up — on Tuesday.'

'Sulikov?' Richard checked.

'Yes,' Harper's breath came erratically; he was panting as he gave his account. 'He said I should have known better, helping myself to the merchandise. He said he'd taken care of Rosa.' He stopped abruptly, wrapping his arms round himself, tucked his hands into his armpits, out of sight, hunched his shoulders. 'I didn't know what he meant at first — she hadn't been found then. She never deserved—' He stopped, licked his lips. 'He said my car had made a lovely blaze. Any more problems, he said, and it'd be my house next, with me in it.'

'Your car was used to carry the body,' Janine reminded him.

'To teach me a lesson.' His eyes glistened. 'I didn't know any of this would happen. Honestly. I thought she would wait — maybe see sense about the baby.'

'An abortion?' she asked.

He looked uneasy.

'You'd no intention of helping her, had you? You were just stalling.'

He didn't answer, he was unnerved and the tic in his jaw was flickering away.

'So, let's see what we've got so far,' she looked at Harper then at Richard. 'You manage the Topcat Club and the brothel in Openshaw. Both businesses are owned by Konrad Sulikov. Sulikov is also behind a trafficking operation. Rosa Milicz was one of the women he smuggled over. You began a sexual relationship with her.' Harper sat there as though exhausted; she wasn't even sure whether he was taking in what she was saying now. 'You arranged for Rosa to dance at the club although she continued to live at the brothel. When Rosa discovered she was pregnant she talked about wanting to return to Poland. You've told us that you last saw Rosa on Sunday at work when you argued about her plans. She was desperate to go back but you told her to wait. On Monday evening you reported your car stolen from home. Tuesday you received a phone call from Konrad Sulikov telling you he had taken care of Rosa and threatening you.'

Harper began to shake.

There was a sharp rap at the door which made them all jump. Richard spoke for the machine: 'Interview suspended, 16.47,' and stopped the tape. Janine went to see who it was, her head still buzzing with the details of Harper's account. His story so far meshed with Marta's; both pointed to Sulikov as the man behind the killing.

Richard followed her out. Butchers was there, his face bright with excitement. He held out a hands-free phone. 'Lee Stone on the phone for you, boss.'

Her heart began to thud. She took the phone, walked a few paces down the corridor. 'Mr Stone, this is DCI Lewis.'

'Jez Gleason. I didn't kill him. I never killed nobody. I need protection, a new identity, the lot.'

She locked eyes with Richard as she listened.

'Where are you?'

'Can you do it, get me a safe house?'

'It's possible. You'd need to come in and talk to me. We'd need to know how you could help us. Where are you Lee?'

'You're tracing this call aren't you . . .'

'No, wait. Please, Lee . . .' He'd hung up already, the dialling tone loud in her ear.

Janine closed her eyes, released her shoulders, swore with frustration. 'He thought we were tracing it,' she told Richard. 'He claims he's innocent.'

Richard looked askance.

'Wants witness protection.'

'He'll ring again,' Richard reassured her.

He probably would but there was no guaranteeing it. Janine wondered whether there was any other way she could have handled the call that would have stopped him freaking out.

'The guy's on the run,' Richard said, 'his name's on posters all over the place, we want to talk to him about two murders and a death by dangerous driving, of course he's paranoid.'

'He must think he's got something to bargain with.'

'He probably thinks telling us about the trafficking will cut it.'

Janine shook her head. 'He'll need a lot more than that. And if he did kill Rosa or Gleason, witness protection won't touch him.'

* * *

Marta's head ached. She wondered if the police would give her something for the pain. They were still in the cells at the police station. The police woman had told them they would be taken to a detention centre later that night. Zofia was weeping, worried that her family would find out exactly what work she had really been doing; she had told them she was waitressing.

'They don't need to know,' Marta told her. 'Just stick to your story, there was a mistake with the paperwork. You don't have to go home anyway.' The girl glanced at her.

'They'll probably dump us at Warsaw airport, get us to talk to the police to see what we know. After that — well . . .'

'What will you say?' Zofia swallowed.

Marta shrugged. 'As little as possible.'

Marta had no intention of staying in Poland. She'd find a way back to the West. But not with the same set-up. She wanted to put as much distance as possible between herself and Sulikov, she knew that much. Harper had always warned them that his boss wouldn't tolerate anyone causing problems. She'd heard the rumours: the girl who'd run away without paying her full fee, who'd been found and locked in with hungry dogs; the undercover police informant who had been strung from a lamp-post, his tongue posted to his widow. Knowing what he was capable of, Marta had never imagined Rosa would be reckless enough to run away.

She'd hoped that Harper would talk her round, force her to abort the baby.

How had Sulikov found out? Had Harper betrayed her? Marta wouldn't put it past him. The way he spoke about Sulikov, he was just as fearful of the man as the rest of them.

The place was too warm. Her skin was sticky, her eyes gritty and the pulsing pain in her temples was getting worse. They had been given tea in plastic cups — it tasted disgusting — and little sandwiches with bitter lettuce and shiny, bland cheese. The custody sergeant had asked whether any of them needed to see a doctor. A precise note was made of their possessions, pitiful really, and their details had been taken. Marta wondered whether they would get anything back. Especially her savings. If this had happened back home, it would already be lining someone's pocket.

It was noisy; there were no carpets or curtains to soak up the noise. Everything echoed off the hard surfaces. The other two were chattering away now in Polish and beyond that Marta could hear other voices, doors banging, bursts of laughter, phones and the whine of a power drill.

The policewoman had gone. She had a nice manner. Not overly officious or trying to bully Marta for answers. She left space instead, tempting you to fill it in. Some of the questions she had asked made Marta think they were close to catching Konrad Sulikov. When the woman talked about giving evidence against him Marta's insides turned to water. Marta had avoided the detective's eyes. She couldn't do that. Not even for Rosa. It would be like putting her head in a noose. Besides, it wouldn't help Rosa now, would it?

Marta stared at the wall, painted speckled blue and grey, graffiti gouged out of it. Danny 4eva, Stan 03/03/03. Someone had drawn a heart in blood; it looked like blood, reddish-brown and smeary.

* * *

Harper was subdued when they resumed the interview. His ashen complexion and continued breathlessness indicated he was still badly shaken. Janine wanted to get as much from him as she could before his solicitor called a halt. 'How did Konrad Sulikov find out that Rosa was running away?'

Harper shook his head. 'I don't know.'

Janine stared at him until he became defensive. 'I didn't tell him,' he protested. She wasn't sure whether she believed him. 'Who else then? He must have found out somehow.'

'I don't know,' he insisted.

'Could it have been Lee Stone?'

'Possibly,' he said slowly. He thought for a moment. He appeared confused. He pinched at the bony bridge on his nose, screwed his eyes shut in concentration. 'When Rosa and I were arguing on Sunday he was waiting to lock up. He might have heard us.' He didn't sound very certain.

'Would he have been able to work out what the argument was about?'

'Erm, maybe. She was yelling at me, I'm going back, with or without your help, that sort of thing. He could have passed it on.'

'When did you last see Stone?'

'Sunday night.'

'Has he contacted you since?'

'No.'

'What is Stone's relationship to Sulikov?' Richard asked him.

'Sulikov was grooming him for the big time.'

'The big time?'

'Sulikov started out with a two-up two-down brothel in Leeds. He's got a bloody empire now: places in Liverpool, Birmingham, London, clubs, escort agencies. He's bringing in girls every month. Some of them working, some of them paying more so they can disappear. He needs people like Stone.'

'Muscle?'

'No limits,' the tic jumped again.

'Could Stone have killed Rosa for Sulikov?'

Harper shook his head, looking lost. He seemed reluctant to accuse the bouncer. Janine was intrigued. She'd have expected Harper to go the whole hog, incriminating others to prove his own innocence but perhaps he wasn't sure and had some shred of integrity left.

'My client can't comment.' The solicitor at least didn't want any idle speculation going on.

Janine rephrased her question. 'Did you hear or see anything that makes you think Stone may have acted on Sulikov's say-so?'

'Lee Stone took my car,' he said, 'though I didn't know that at the time. Then Sulikov rang me about it.'

'This phone call after your car was stolen — where did Sulikov ring you from?' said Richard.

'His mobile. I don't know exactly where.'

'Poland?' Richard pressed him.

'No.' Harper hesitated then added, 'erm. . .he's been over in the UK this week.'

Janine felt her heart punch; there was a batting sensation in her head. 'What?' she demanded. Her skin tightened with apprehension.

'He's been over here.' Harper shuffled uncomfortably.

Unbelievable! All along they had assumed the man was on the continent and Harper had left it till now to disabuse them of this notion. Still trying to thwart their investigation? 'Why the hell didn't you tell us this?' she shouted, 'you think he killed Rosa but you're still protecting him.'

'I . . .' he couldn't answer. He blinked. The tic flickered.

'Where's he staying?'

'I don't know,' he said dismissively, a little too quickly for Janine's liking.

'Where?' Richard had picked up on it too.

'Please, I can't,' his voice wavered.

She stared at him, restrained herself from raising her voice and used a steely tone instead. 'Your silence has done enough damage already, now answer the question.'

'He'll know I told you. You've no idea what he's like.' Harper was becoming hysterical, his face contorted and reddening.

'We'll be discreet,' she said.

'Discreet! He's a fucking maniac!' Harper yelled, half out of his seat. 'He'll kill me.'

'We've enough to arrest him, we'll put him behind bars,' she said. 'Now you can help us or we can put you there with him, too. Your choice.'

Harper sank back, rubbing his face, trying to calm his breathing. He was very agitated.

Come on. Janine willed him, her heart beating hard. She knew without this they'd lose Sulikov; soon as he heard about the raid on the brothel he'd disappear. It wouldn't be impossible to pursue him in Poland but it would be a lot more haphazard. He was here, in the country, under their noses. 'Mr Harper?'

He blew a breath out, pressed the tips of his fingers to his temples. Bracing himself. His shoulders slumped and Janine knew she had won. 'He's at The Midland Hotel, Crowne Plaza. He's probably left by now,' he added feebly.

And you hope he has, Janine thought. Harper's cowardice ran all the way through him like print through a stick of Blackpool rock. He was a weak man. Even Marta had shown more guts in telling them about Sulikov.

CHAPTER NINETEEN

The Midland was one of the ritziest hotels in town. Janine and Pete had spent a weekend there in their courting days. The café and restaurant were popular meeting places and the doormen in their black top hats and red livery gave a classy feel to the place.

The receptionist, whose face fell with consternation when she saw their police identification, confirmed that Mr Sulikov was staying there. 'Polish gentleman. He checked in Wednesday evening.'

'Wednesday? Not earlier?' Janine was puzzled. Rosa had been killed on Monday. Where had Sulikov been that night, or on the Tuesday? Visiting other parts of his operation? Leaving the dirty work to Stone?

'He's still here?' she asked.

'That's right.'

Relief sluiced through her — they weren't too late.

'Is he in his room, now?' asked Richard.

The receptionist turned to check the keys, then back to them shaking her head and Janine felt a lurch of disappointment.

Janine told her they needed to see the room; the woman got someone to cover the reception desk while she took them up in the lift.

Shap was just arriving as they went into the room. While the receptionist watched, Janine, Richard and Shap examined the place. It barely looked occupied: a hold-all at the foot of the bed, ruffled covers and a small toilet bag in the bathroom the only signs that Sulikov was staying there. Shap riffled through the bag in search of any documents but it held only clothes.

'Travels light,' Janine observed, finding it hard to keep the frustration from her voice. Too impatient, she chided herself. At least now we know where he is we've a damn good chance of picking him up which is a much better state than we were in three hours ago.

Janine spoke to the receptionist. 'We'll be leaving Sergeant Shap here to wait for Mr Sulikov. He can sit in the lobby. Now, if you can let him know once Mr Sulikov is back, other officers will be on standby and we'll make sure there's as little disruption as possible. And please don't mention our visit, to anyone.'

The receptionist nodded, wide-eyed, keen to help.

Janine looked at Shap. 'And as soon as Sulikov steps in that lift I want to know.'

Shap nodded. 'My pleasure, boss.'

Driving back, Janine aired her thoughts with Richard. 'He didn't check in until Wednesday — where was he Monday night when Rosa was killed?'

'No idea. Staying somewhere else? Upped sticks to try and cover his tracks?' Richard braked. The traffic on Deansgate was backed up. 'We'd have been quicker walking,' he pointed out.

'Raining, though,' Janine said. 'You got a brolly?'

'Don't believe in 'em.'

'The Lemon'll love this.' She stared out at the passers-by, 'Two suspects both nowhere to be seen.'

'We're close though, to Sulikov, at least. Run him to earth. Just a question of waiting for him to come back. We're winning.'

'You reckon?' She looked at him, seeking reassurance. She was glad she was working with Richard, someone she trusted enough to be able to voice her doubts.

'Don't you?' He was beginning to look tired, his complexion paler, smudged under his eyes. He was careful about his appearance, always well groomed, his clothes impeccable but no amount of tending could remove the signs of a tough case. It was getting to him like it had to her.

'Yeah, you're probably right. It's like transition in labour.'

Richard frowned.

'Lowest point, you've been at it for hours, you just want to give up and go home, but then it all kicks off. You don't have any sense of how close you really are.'

'Thanks for that,' he pulled a face. 'But it's not a comparison I really want to run with.'

* * *

As the security van transported them from Manchester to the holding centre in Yorkshire, Marta looked out at the night and the rain and the lights that edged the motorway. The last time she'd ridden anywhere it had been her journey into the UK from Poland. After that, it had been like living under curfew. They stayed in the house; the phone only took incoming calls.

Once she'd started at Topcat, Rosa had more freedom than the others. Loverboy Harper trusted her. She got the bus to work and now and then she called at the shops in town to get a little treat for her housemates. She would bring flowers if it was a person's name day or good shampoo and conditioner, nice make-up for them to share.

Occasionally the girls at the brothel got tips and they would share them out. The best tipper was a man called Barry. He was very rough and said horrible things; you had to pretend to cry and then he'd really beat you but afterwards he'd be nice as pie and leave an extra £10 note.

Sometimes a girl would get moved. Sulikov had other places and girls would be sent there without much warning.

Whenever Lee Stone brought anyone new Mr Harper would be around a lot, keeping an eye on things, explaining the benefit of accepting the situation and getting on with it.

'We don't want any trouble, do we?' he'd say. Half threat, half reassurance.

Marta remembered her first night in the country. They'd docked at Hull and, just outside the town, they had been left to wait for a different minibus. It had been freezing, not snowy like home, just a bitter east wind that sliced through their clothes. They had waited for over an hour. When the bus arrived, the driver, Lee Stone, demanded twenty pounds from them for the fare. 'We've paid for the journey already,' Marta said.

'Not this stretch. Cough up or stay here.'

They didn't all follow his words but his gestures made the choice quite plain. He wouldn't take zlotys. Some of them had changed money on the ferry He took it from them, grinning like a dog with two dicks.

It had been late afternoon as they got on the road again. The light was fading. Much of the landscape was flat, like at home. Then they had joined the motorway which climbed up into huge hills. No trees on the top, just bare grasslands, sheep here and there and regular towns in the valleys.

There was music on the radio and once or twice Marta felt a thrill of achievement. She was here. She'd made it.

She had read the signs: Leeds, Huddersfield, Oldham, Salford and wondered about pronunciation. Manchester was huge, lit by orange streetlamps. Not pretty like Krakow. Everyone had heard of Manchester. Manchester United, David Beckham and Oasis.

When the minibus had turned off a side road and stopped at an unlit shed, her heart sank. They were near a river; the headlights caught the slick of water by a quay of some sort. Was this where they had to stay? She had heard stories of people sleeping in garages and derelict warehouses. A door banged in the wind but the driver made no move to make them leave their seats.

Marta peered out. You'd never dream you were so close to the city; there were no lighted windows, no signs of life.

'What for are we waiting?' She knew the English wasn't quite right but it was the best she could do.

'Transfers,' the man pulled a paper from his pocket, flicked on an overhead light. 'Six going on to London.'

London! Marta's heart quickened. London would be even better. A good place to disappear once she had saved enough money.

But when another van arrived that driver pointed to six of the other girls and waved them out of their seats to go with him. The London girls were told to give their passports to the new man. They exchanged hasty goodbyes with Marta, Zofia and Petra and wished each other luck.

Lee Stone drove them to the house and Harper had met them there. The place had recently been painted and carpeted. It smelled of cheap gloss and glue and mildew.

There was an older woman there too. She had orange dyed hair, a large bust and a wheezy voice. Her fingers were thick with rings. Mr Harper introduced her as Josie. Josie would show them the ropes, get them settled in. They should get a good night's sleep. Tomorrow there would be a party. Some of Mr Harper's friends were coming over, keen to meet the girls.

Marta had felt her smile waver and noticed the flutter of nerves in the other girls' responses.

'Where are we doing the dancing?' Zofia had asked.

'Here darling,' Josie had said. 'And tomorrow we'll sort you out with some nice new costumes.'

Marta closed her eyes. Her head still pounded and she felt sick to the stomach. No one had told them when they would be sent back to Poland. Probably Rosa's remains would be sent back, too, so her family could bury her in the local churchyard.

If she got a chance Marta would call home; a night or two to see her own parents, find out how they were getting along. And then? She'd find out whether people could get her into Berlin or maybe Rome? Or London, she still fancied London and her English was much better now.

She looked again as the security van left the motorway and braked at a large roundabout. She stared at her own reflection in the glass, into her own eyes. London, she promised herself, next time I'll make it to London.

* * *

Back at base, Janine and Richard checked in with the incident room.

'Nothing from the airlines,' said Richard. They were trying to establish when and how Sulikov had entered the country.

'Maybe he drove. We'll try the ports?'

'Yes.' Janine checked her watch. If she left now she could call at the shopping centre for essentials on the way back, get home more or less when she'd promised. 'Take Harper's statement,' she said to Richard. 'DNA swab as well. And bail him to return here first thing in the morning.'

Halfway round the mini-mart, with a thrill of panic, Janine remembered Charlotte's appointment. Today! She had meant to cancel. Damn! She paid for the nappies and the crisps and the hair conditioner and on the way back to her car she scrolled through her phone directory for the doctor's number.

She pressed call and opened her passenger door, slinging her purchases in. She ended up talking to an answer phone as she walked round to the driver's side. 'She was due in for her developmental review this afternoon, half past two.' Janine opened the door, got into the car. 'I'm really sorry I meant to cancel the appointment.' Leaning forward to start the ignition she felt something cool on her neck. Her hand began to move to brush it away.

'Start the car,' Lee Stone said.

Shock scorched through her, burning her stomach, sending tremors of fear wiring along her arms and into her fingers. A gun at her neck. Cold metal.

'Do exactly what I say.' His face in Janine's rear view mirror.

Janine could smell the man: damp hair from the rain and a mix of nicotine and spice.

'Give me the phone,' he told her, 'and start the car.'

She daren't nod. Anything might prompt him to pull the trigger. She must be very, very careful. She held the phone out, bending her arm back towards him. She felt his hand, surprisingly warm over hers as he took the phone.

Janine turned the key, the engine growled into life.

'Out the car park, and left,' said Stone.

Janine took a breath; her chest hurt, like there were straps tightening round it. She depressed the clutch, selected first gear and touched the accelerator. Slowly the car moved off.

Stone sat back, lowering the weapon. Janine followed his directions, silent and compliant. She was working at a subconscious, innate level. When she tried to think about what she should be doing, what she had been trained to do in situations like this, her brain clogged up, blanked out. As if the answers were shrouded in white candy floss, too sticky to get through. She had distanced herself from the situation, focusing only on driving the car, on listening to Stone. Deep down she knew it was the only way, a defence mechanism, because if she had admitted her fear, allowed free rein to her emotions she would have fallen apart, begging and crying and generally mucking it all up. She could do that later. For now she would trust her reactions and the powerful, overwhelming instinct for self-preservation.

* * *

Pete was growing more and more impatient as he waited for Janine to get back. OK. she had a big case on, but she had promised to let him know if she was going to be any later than expected. He didn't mind hanging on longer but she could have the courtesy to warn him. He didn't know whether to ring Tina now or whether Janine was about to waltz in the door at any moment. He checked his watch again. Sod it! He rang her mobile but she didn't answer. He tried her work number.

'Hello? DI Mayne.'

Pete would have preferred it if someone else had answered. Janine spent all her time with Richard and he knew the pair of them were good friends. He wondered sometimes if there was more to it. The thought made his jaw tense up.

'Richard, it's Pete.'

'Ah.' No mistaking the coolness in Mayne's tone.

'Is Janine there?'

'She's gone.'

'She said she'd be back by now.'

'Have you tried her mobile?'

'Yes,' Pete snapped, 'she's not answering.'

There was a pause. Then, 'She left an hour ago.'

'An hour?' Concern pricked at Pete's spine. 'She should be home by now.' He didn't like this.

'Right,' Richard suddenly all business, 'I'll put a call out, all units on alert. We'll find her.'

'You'll ring me, soon as you know anything.'

'Of course.'

Any impatience on Pete's part had drained away leaving him swamped by anxiety as he ended the call.

CHAPTER TWENTY

Each time a man entered the lobby, single or accompanied, Shap's eyes flicked over to the receptionist. And so far he had been disappointed. No signal from the girl that here was the quarry. He entertained himself guessing what people were doing here: the smart business types in town to talk up deals; the trendy ones who might be in the media, actors or visiting musicians; and the visitors, here for pleasure, taking in the history or the culture, or the shopping.

He half hoped he'd spot a celebrity — The Midland was a popular meeting spot — maybe someone from Corrie or United; he could add them to his list along with Robbie Williams, David Jason, Victoria Wood and Michael Owen.

Another bloke approached the desk. He had blond hair, wore a long raincoat; he was carrying a laptop. Eyes alert, Shap waited. The way the man stood obscured Shap's view of the girl on the desk. Come on, he thought, let the dog see the rabbit. The man took his key and moved away towards the lift. The receptionist gave a small shake of her head.

Shap sighed and sat back. What was Sulikov up to? Out on the town? They'd a pair of coppers posted at both the club and the brothel with strict instructions to make an arrest if the Polack turned up there. Someone who could afford to stay here could be living the high life: dinner at Simply Heathcoat's, on to one of the city's private members' clubs. Or maybe he was out seeing what his rivals in the sex trade were up to this season, sampling the goods.

The thought made him cross his legs. Mind on the job. He watched a girl go by, nice looker. Mind you the girl behind the desk was quite a stunner, smiled a lot too. But she had laughed outright when he asked if she fancied a drink sometime. Like he'd made a joke. 'Hah, hah, hah. I don't think so,' she'd giggle. Probably engaged, he decided. Not available rather than not interested.

Another bloke came in, grey-haired and stoop shouldered and Shap pretended to read the refreshments menu he was holding, while he watched him ask for his key.

* * *

Stone had directed Janine to drive to an abandoned storage depot within sight of Manchester Airport. Here and there loomed old freight containers, rusting and daubed with graffiti. The rough ground was strewn with weeds and old gravel tracks criss-crossed the area. Janine had never been here before. She wondered how Stone knew about it. Barbed wire surrounded much of the perimeter and she had seen notices which suggested that re-development work was imminent, along with weather-beaten signs warning of guard dog patrols.

After telling her to stop and turn the engine off, Stone had issued his demands. 'I am not going down for murder,' said Stone. 'You've got to tell them. And you've got to get me some protection.'

Janine's voice felt unreliable. 'It doesn't work—' she began.

'Now!' he shouted, making her jump. 'You don't have much choice, do you, lady?'

'Put the gun down. I can't do anything until you put the gun down.'

'No!' His face was contorted.

'Just–'

'Shut it.'

'Please, put the gun down.'

'Shut up.'

'Please, Lee, please put the–'

'Shut up!' He yelled. 'Shut the fuck up!'

There was a powerful crack, a whoomph of air. The front windscreen shattered, lines crazing across the glass. He'd shot the gun.

Janine started to tremble uncontrollably. Her heart thundered against her ribs. Her ears hurt. She had felt the impact of the blast through her bones, in all her soft tissue. Oh, God, help me, she prayed.

Stone still held the gun. She watched in the mirror which was still intact. 'You gonna listen to me?' She could barely make out the words, her ears singing and buzzing.

'Yes,' she said hoarsely.

'Sulikov rang us, on my mobile. He said the girl had died of an overdose. We had to take the car and get rid. We didn't know he'd killed her. Then, well, job like that, putting her in the water, you get all wired up. Needed to burn some of the adrenalin off. But we didn't kill her.'

'But you ran over Ann-Marie.' She regretted the words as soon as they had left her mouth.

'Shut up,' he shouted again. 'Shut up and listen.'

She gripped the steering wheel to stop her hands from shaking.

'When you let us out, I rang Sulikov back. We needed to get right away.' He paused. She saw him blink momentarily, his face drawn and tired in the reflection. She realised he was at breaking point. 'He goes ballistic, yabbering on in Polack, but he knew we'd be bad news hanging round here. He was going back to Poland — says he'll take us across the Channel. There's some warehouses not far from us, an old tunnel. He says he'll meet us at the other side. We go all the way in. He's standing at the top of the steps, yelling at us hurry up. Then he opens up. Fucking Terminator. Jez goes down. I legged it. He's firing after me. Soon as he knows where I am, he'll be after me next. You've got to get me protection.'

'You'll turn Queen's evidence?'

'I dunno.'

'It's a two-way street.'

'He'll get round it. You'll never get him to court. He'll drop out of sight in Europe. Then, what about me? If there's no trial?'

She tried to reassure him, 'With your testimony and stuff we've got from Harper, we've a strong case. We know where Sulikov is. But we need to move quickly.' A sudden swirl of unfairness caught hold of her. She was scared and sick of him threatening her. He wanted to deal — he could do it her way. 'And absolutely nothing happens until you move that bloody gun. Do you know how hard it is to even think straight with you pointing that thing at me?'

'How do I know you're gonna do what you say?'

'You don't. But I'm being straight with you. You give us the information we need on Sulikov and we'll get you into witness protection. As long as it all adds up.'

He lowered the gun. 'What now?'

She felt like weeping. She cleared her throat, the sound was strange in her ears. 'Now I take you in.' She pressed her hands to her face, trying to calm herself. She rubbed at her forehead, rolled back her shoulders.

Movement caught her eye. On the horizon, where they had entered the field, a string of police cars appeared in view and among them Richard's car. Oh, bloody Nora, Janine thought. It's *Thelma and Louise.*

'It's a set-up!' Stone screamed and raised the gun again.

'No,' Janine insisted. 'Let me talk to them. I'll send them away.'

'You conned me!'

'No! Lee, I didn't, you've got to believe me. I'll tell them.' Without waiting for permission she switched on the police radio, activated the amplifier and spoke into the handset, 'Richard, back off! Back off now! Get them all out of here.'

The line crackled then Richard's voice. 'Are you OK, Janine? Are you hurt?'

'Never better.' Her sarcasm felt white hot. 'Lee Stone is coming in. But only if you get rid of the bloody cavalry.'

'Are you sure you're not hurt? We've had reports of gunfire.'

Listen to me, you fool, she thought. 'Ten out of ten, Richard! And I'm the one with bloody hearing loss not you. Back off!' she said clearly, fury tightening every syllable. 'Back off. Now! We do not need an escort. Mr Stone will require legal services and complete protection. We will be treating him as a valuable witness. Now clear the area. That's not a suggestion, that's a bloody order!'

Seconds passed and then Richard replied. 'Understood. You'll follow us back?'

'Yes.'

The convoy left. The lights still flaring. She prayed they wouldn't try anything clever. An ambush or a roadblock. That they would trust what she had said and let her keep her promise.

'OK,' she told Stone. 'Let's try that again.'

He nodded curtly. 'I need your gun.'

He hesitated for a moment then passed it to her. It was heavy. She wrapped it and put it safely away. Then, her mus-cles throbbing with tension, she used the ice-scraper to clear the remaining glass from the windscreen, pushing it onto the bonnet.

She felt a surge of self-pity. She wanted to be home and safe and warm, not here with some lunatic who would shoot her as soon as look at her. Just do the job, she told herself. Get on with it. She had to stay strong, and practical and level-headed.

Her limbs juddering, she started the car. Haltingly she drove, concentrating fiercely and shivering in cold rain that spattered on her face. Other drivers slowed, seeing the damage. Twice she stalled, cursing as she fired the ignition again, her fingers feeling swollen and clumsy.

Stone said nothing. Did nothing.

* * *

They were all waiting outside the station: Richard, Butchers, DCs and loads of uniforms. She'd no doubt there were marksmen somewhere but at least they'd had the wits to keep them out of view.

'I'm going to get out first and then I want you to get out slowly,' Janine told Stone.

'I need to cuff you,' she said, when he complied. 'They won't let us in unless you're in restraints.'

He looked at her, still distrustful. Then he relented, held out his hands. She put on the flexicuffs, clumsily, hampered by the way her own hands were still quivering.

At that point a number of uniformed officers walked forward to escort Lee Stone into the building. Richard approached Janine. He studied her for a long moment, unsmiling, his eyes guileless. She matched his stare. Then he gave a tiny smile, closed his eyes in relief. 'Where's the gun?'

'Glove compartment, in the nappy sack.'

Richard began to speak, no doubt about to make a quip.

'Don't,' she said. She wasn't ready yet. She needed to get into the building and find somewhere to collapse.

As soon as Stone had been taken away, Janine fled to the toilets. She sat down in one of the stalls and put her head in her hands. The shaking grew stronger; it felt as though there was a boulder in her throat, lead in her belly. She could smell the stink of cordite on her clothes, and her own fear. A wave of rage sluiced through her, impotent, blazing rage. She balled her fists and banged at her own knees, cursing repeatedly. Slagging off Stone, the job, the world that had placed her in such danger.

She finally allowed herself to think about her kids, about them waiting for her at home. And then of Ann-Marie's home: the little girl would never come in the door again, never giggle at the telly or complain about her food or sing. It was that that undid her. She cried noisily and messily until she felt cleansed.

When she came out to wash her face, her nose was swollen and red, her face puffy. She splashed cold water over it repeatedly then patted it dry and brushed her hair.

She saw the custody sergeant and promised him a full written statement for the morning. 'I really need to get home now, Geoff,' she croaked.

'You go. No problem.'

Richard was in the incident room. She leaned on the door frame and gave him a wave.

'Hey,' he said softly, 'nice one.'

She bit her lip, keeping control. 'I'm off. If you need me . . .'

'I know where you are, he said.

'How'd you find us?' the thought struck her.

'We'd an all points alert out. An unmarked patrol saw you leaving Royle Green Road. They called in your location when you went into the fields.'

'Who's doing the interview?'

'I am.'

She gave him a summary of what Stone had told her.

'Think he's telling the truth?'

She exhaled noisily, shaking her head. 'Ask me tomorrow.'

CHAPTER TWENTY-ONE

Pete didn't say a word when she walked in. Just hugged her, held her close. Even that hurt, made her bloody eyes water. Thoughts of how many years that hug had been hers alone, well — hers and the kids. Pre-Tina. His body so familiar. She knew him so well but then maybe she hadn't known him at all. Certainly not well enough to realise he was being unfaithful. She pulled away.

Pete poured her a generous brandy, handed it to her.

She took a mouthful, the taste reminding her of Christmas. She savoured the warmth in her mouth before letting it slide down her throat.

'The kids?'

'Just think you're working late.'

She nodded, relieved that she wouldn't have to reassure them. Deal with their own fear as well as her own.

'How did he get in the car?' Pete asked.

She exhaled. 'He's a professional car thief, among other things. He could get into anything.'

Pete shook his head, his tongue balled into the corner of his mouth. 'Pete, I'm all right.'

He nodded ruefully. 'I want to know what happened, all of it.'

She told him. It helped to recount it, to go over each memory: the moment in the car park when she'd felt the chill of metal on her neck, the visceral threat of Stone's violence, the horrendously loud retort of the gun going off and a split-second when she thought he had shot her; that she'd die in the car, on wasteland; that she wouldn't hold Charlotte again or see Michael or the others, that they'd have to grow up without her; the panic of the posse arriving, just as she thought she had defused the situation; Stone's explosion of rage and her frantic attempts to stop Richard and the others, to save herself. Then the worst part really, when she knew that she had survived it, when she was no longer acting purely on instinct and the need to hold it all together, when she could finally let go and release all the emotions, the bright anger that made her teeth ache, the bowel-churning terror that scuttled across her skin and through her veins, the sorrow at what she had endured and the huge need to be comforted, to be loved and cherished. To be safe and to celebrate life in all its precious fragility.

Now and again Pete interrupted but only to clarify events for himself. Mostly he just listened, nodding when she sought reassurance, echoing her sense of shock when things had been most critical. When she had finished he hugged her again. 'I've never been so scared,' he admitted.

'Well, I'm here now.' She drew back. 'In one piece, more or less. He was wound up that tight, Pete, I should have taken more time to calm him down.'

'Christ, Janine, you're not blaming yourself?'

'No, just figuring out what I'd do different.'

'Next time?' His face grew pale, a sign of anger.

'No! Possibly! But he wasn't there trying to hurt me — he was giving himself up.'

'I don't want there to be a next time,' Pete said. 'I couldn't bear it.' He squeezed her hand.

'Me neither,' she tried to smile. It was late, she was spent. Battered physically and emotionally. Janine took another swig. 'You'd better go.'

'Yeah?' His voice suddenly softer. His eyes were burning into hers. He wasn't just asking about this evening.

There was a pause. Janine's stomach flipped over. It would be so easy to just give in, to feel his arms around her. The familiar smell of him, the feel of his lips, the shorthand of communication that they'd built over all the years. But when she tried to imagine Pete actually coming back, back in the house, back in her bed, she couldn't. He'd hurt her, so very deeply, the last year had been the hardest in her life. Any love she had for him now was tainted by that.

'I can't . . . we can't go back. I couldn't . . .' What? She thought. Do it, trust you, face it going wrong again — all of the above? '. . . after everything . . . it's too late . . .'

'The kids . . .'

'We've still got the kids, Pete. We're lucky.'

His face fell, he twisted away, then back. For a moment she thought he might argue with her but instead he just said, 'I'm sorry. Oh, Janine, I'm sorry.' She could hear the passion in his apology, his voice cracking. She believed him. He really was sorry. So was she. But sorry didn't make it all better.

Then he held her again and she squeezed her eyes tight to contain the tears and wished for the thousandth time that they could turn the clock back. That things could be as they were, that he'd never cheated on her, left her, ruined it all.

When he had gone she ran a shower, washing her hair and her body, turning the water very hot until she was breathless, then a shot of cold. She pulled on comfortable clothes, towelled her hair dry. Then, with exquisite bad timing, Charlotte woke up.

* * *

The dog nudged at Chris's leg, after food. He pulled himself up and found a tin in the cupboard, spooned out the meat and put it down. The dog got stuck in.

It was Debbie who had pushed to get a dog. Ann-Marie had been five at the time. Debbie had developed fibroids and the pain and bleeding had become so severe that the consultant recommended a hysterectomy. No more children.

Debbie fretted about Ann-Marie being an only child. 'I don't want her spoilt,' she had said, 'thinking she's the be-all and end-all.'

'She is the be-all and end-all,' he'd protested.

She dug him in the ribs. 'You know what I mean.'

'You don't want her spoilt but you want to buy her a dog. What's next, a pony?'

'Chris!'

'Debbie, she's fine. She gets on all right at school, a lot better at sharing than some of them, by all accounts. She sees her cousins. A dog would want walking and vets' bills and all sorts.'

She let it go then but not for long. Dropping canine hints into the conversation. How a dog would be great for exercise, how so-and-so down the road had got a lovely mongrel from the Dogs' Home. He feigned disinterest, mentioned hairs everywhere and worming tablets. Meanwhile he'd called on a mate whose wife ran a kennels in Reddish. They knew someone who wanted a good home for a young dog. House trained but they'd discovered the grandson had a bad allergy.

He took Ann-Marie with him; told her they had to collect something for work.

She started at first when the dog came forward and sniffed her hand. She pursed her lips and blinked hard but stood her ground.

'You can stroke him,' the owner said. Ann-Marie put her hand on the dog's neck and rubbed it gently.

'He's called Tiger.'

'What sort is he?' she asked.

'He's liquorice.'

Ann-Marie frowned.

'All sorts,' the man said.

Chris laughed but she didn't get the reference.

She patted the dog's back.

'He likes that,' Chris told her. 'Shall we take him home?'

She glanced at him, her mind alert to adult teasing. But he nodded.

'Yes?' he said. 'To keep?'

Delight bloomed on her face. 'Yes!' She clapped her hands and Tiger barked.

He couldn't cry. There was sand behind his eyes, heavy, hot, dry sand. A desert.

'Daddy,' her voice jolted him. Shock sparking through his blood. He looked up sharply, his spine crawling. She stood in the doorway, her hands on her hips, her tracksuit trousers on, the ones with the zips and her stripy pink and blue sweater. There was a smudge of biro on one cheek and an orange smear at the corner of her mouth. She must have had beans for lunch, or hoops. 'It's a bit messy.' She frowned at the state of the kitchen.

He nodded. His heart blocked his throat, his vision tilted.

'Tiger wants a walk,' she said. He stared at her.

'Come on, then,' she said impatiently.

He stood clumsily, grabbed the lead from the hook, keeping his eyes locked on her. The dog, hearing the chink of chain, skittered round the kitchen, winding its body to and fro in anticipation.

Chris opened the back door and the dog darted through. Ann-Marie stepped out afterwards. Chris followed, bent to fit the lead on Tiger and, as he straightened, Ann-Marie slipped her hand into his.

When they got back, the dog shook itself, rain spangled everywhere. Chris hung up his jacket, regarded the clutter. He moved the pots to the dishwasher, opened the cupboard under the sink and got out the dustpan and brush. His face was wet, tears dripping steadily from his nose as he laboured, small huffs of breath shook his shoulders.

He heard Debbie coming downstairs and wiped one sleeve across his eyes, the other across his nose.

She stood in the doorway, her arms wrapped about her waist. 'The police rang, they've arrested Lee Stone.'

He felt his shoulders drop, the crash of relief. Still kneeling, avoiding her gaze.

'Chris, there are things we have to do. The registrars, for the death certificate, the funeral home . . .' she spoke with effort and he could tell she was fighting emotion. Being practical. 'I can't do this on my own.'

He bobbed his head. 'We'll go first thing.'

He heard a little sharp exhalation — she'd been holding her breath, her turn now for relief.

'Debbie,' he halted, his tongue thick, the words like broken stones in his mouth. 'I can't . . . don't, don't want to talk,' he managed.

'OK.'

'Just get through this.' He meant the funeral.

He would come and sit at her side while they watched the registrar use a fountain pen to meticulously enter the facts of their daughter's death. He would make sure he had cash from the ATM to pay for their copy of the certificate. He would drive with Debbie to the undertakers and choose a coffin and listen while she talked about what clothes they wanted her to be dressed in and when the viewing would be and special mementoes they wanted to put in the coffin. 'We,' she would say but in his silence Chris would leave it all up to her. Because none of it mattered. He would stand with her while the small coffin slid from view, shake hands with the rest of the family, the teachers, acknowledge the children's flowers and poems. He would listen while she dictated the text for the memorial stone. Sit beside her as they were driven home. Walk the dog.

And after all that . . . he really didn't know. Was there anything left between them but grief? Could he ever look her in the eye again? Forgive her as Ann-Marie had forgiven him? Forgive himself? He simply didn't know.

CHAPTER TWENTY-TWO

At the station, Stone repeated his version of events in the formal setting of the interview room. Butchers accompanied Richard. The duty solicitor, who had been hoping for a quiet night in with a video, looked half asleep. Stone had exchanged his own clothes for overalls and had been fingerprinted and swabbed for DNA. He answered all the questions they put to him.

'Sulikov rang you on Monday at 7.15. What exactly did he say?' Richard asked.

'There was a problem. One of the girls had OD'd . . . we needed to dispose of her. He said to pick the car up at eight near these units in Burnage.'

'You got the car from Harper's, didn't you?' Richard checked.

'What?' Stone frowned. 'No. I mean it's Harper's car, bet he wasn't too happy about it.'

'But you didn't get it from his place?'

Stone got prickly. 'I told you, Burnage, industrial units,' he sighed and shook his head as though they were beyond belief. He spoke slowly as if dealing with a dozy child, 'the keys were in the ignition, dosh in the glove compartment, body in the boot.'

'Then what?'

'We take it to the place at the river. Get rid of the body.'

'And after?' Richard cocked his head.

'Went for a drive.'

'All night?'

'Pretty much. Stopped off a couple of places. Don't remember exactly.'

'Why's that then?'

'Wasn't exactly sober,' Stone sneered.

'Those your orders were they?'

He scowled. 'Sulikov said to torch the car. Nice set of wheels, seemed a shame to do that before we'd put it through its paces.'

'And Ann-Marie?' Richard said quietly.

Stone's eyes flicked away and back. 'Jez lost control, just an accident.'

'You saying Gleason was driving?' Butchers asked. A nod.

'We need a yes,' Butchers signalled to the tape.

'Yes,' he hissed.

'Funny that,' Richard said, 'you letting him drive, hard man like you. Thought you'd want to stay behind the wheel.'

Stone said nothing.

'So, Rosa?' Richard sat back surveying the man. 'When you opened the boot what did you find?'

Stone shifted in his seat. 'She were all wrapped up. Couldn't even tell who it was.'

'Was she stiff? Was she warm?'

'For God's sake,' Stone squirmed.

'Hard facts, Mr Stone. We need to know when she died, we need to know where.'

'Don't ask me,' he complained.

'We are asking you. What state was the body in?'

'She were just — heavy,' he managed.

Richard switched tack again. 'Mr Sulikov, you saw him shoot Gleason?'

'Yeah.'

'In cold blood.'

'Yeah.'

'Gleason provoke him in any way?'

'No.'

'Can you describe the weapon?'

'No. It was dark, hardly see a thing. There's this loud bang and Jez went down. I legged it.'

'You'd no idea you were walking into a trap?'

'No. Sulikov calls, you jump.'

'He over here much?'

'I don't know, first time I've seen him but look, I'm a bouncer, I'm a fixer. I'm not in on the board meetings or the fancy meals or the wheeling and dealing. Bloke like that, he keeps his distance; a call, that's all it takes. He sits in his bloody Polish castle or whatever and dials a number. He's people like me to do his dirty work, he doesn't need to get down in the muck with the rest of us.'

'That a plea for sympathy?'

Stone snorted and folded his arms.

* * *

When Richard rang, Janine had just sorted Tom (and the ever-present Frank) out with juice and some dried fruit and was trying to get Charlotte dressed again after changing her nappy. She put Charlotte back on the changing mat and picked up the phone.

'Have you got Sulikov?' she demanded, full of anticipation.

'No. Hasn't been back to the hotel yet.'

Janine felt the cold wash of disappointment.

'But Stone's version stands up,' Richard told her. 'Negative on the DNA, the skin sample under Rosa's nails wasn't his — must be Sulikov's. Something's a bit off, though,' Richard's tone changed, 'Stone claims they picked the Mercedes up on the street, an industrial estate, in Burnage, at eight o'clock. Sulikov told them where it was.'

'Burnage,' something clicked in Janine's memory. 'Wasn't there a sighting that didn't fit?'

'Yes — teenager who'd seen the car there around that time.'

'None of this makes sense,' she complained. She ran her fingers through her hair. 'Think about it. Sulikov hears that Rosa is going to run away, perhaps Harper lets it slip, so he decides to make an example of her and he kills her. Then there's all the palaver with the bin bags; trying to make her unrecognisable. Hoping we'll never find her. Then what does Sulikov do? He goes to Harper's house, steals Harper's car, brings it back to wherever Rosa is. He puts the body in the boot, then he drives the car to Burnage and leaves it for Stone to pick up. Why on earth do that?'

'To teach Harper a lesson like he said?'

'But why do it himself? Why not get Stone to do it? Stealing cars is right up his street. Sulikov would have to leave the body to go off to Harper's to steal the car.' She had another thought, 'Unless she was killed at Harper's house?'

'They could be in it together,' Richard suggested.

Had both men killed Rosa and then colluded in the cover up? But Harper had ratted on his boss. When they caught up with Sulikov would he blame Harper in turn? Marta had told Janine that Harper was a weak man. Had he betrayed his girlfriend to Sulikov? Rosa had gone out that Monday afternoon, maybe Harper had lured her to his house. Then left her to Sulikov. Afterwards they wanted Stone to dispose of the body but didn't want to link it to Harper's house.

'I think we should get a search warrant for Harper's house,' Janine said.

Charlotte crooned and cycled her legs.

'I still can't work out why Sulikov got so involved,' Janine continued. 'We know he's got a fearsome reputation. Everyone's scared stiff of him. He's got an empire — goons to do his every bidding. He keeps it all at arm's length — that makes sense to anyone with half a brain. It's the likes of Stone and Gleason who do the dirty work, take the falls.'

'Maybe–'

'Oh, Tom!' He'd knocked his drink over the table. Janine dived for a cloth.

'Wasn't me, it was Frank.' Tom said quickly.

She mopped at the pool.

'Wait,' she said to Richard, trying to follow her train of thought. 'All that stuff about giving Stone and Gleason a lift over the Channel — does that sound likely? Mr Big turned taxi driver.'

'But he wasn't going to drive them anywhere — it was an ambush; we know that. Wanted them dead.'

'Why kill them himself?'

There was a pause. 'Enhance his reputation,' he suggested.

'He wasn't usually hands on.' Janine rubbed at her forehead; there was something missing, just out of grasp, tucked away in her mind.

Janine stared at Tom sitting beside the imaginary Frank, sharing out raisins. Wasn't me, it was Frank. Shifting the blame. Just like Harper who had blamed everything on Sulikov. A chill washed through Janine and her heart began to hammer. Harper, Sulikov. Could she be right? 'Oh, God!' she said urgently. 'Richard, the photo of Sulikov. Has it arrived?'

'Not yet.'

'Get onto Poland and tell them to email it to me immediately — here. And double check Harper's ID.'

She paced up and down waiting for the message to come through, her guts knotted, her face feeling aflame.

The familiar tone sounded. You have mail. One message and an attachment. She clicked on the message and watched it open. Richard was still on the line, watching at his end.

'Got it,' Janine said, her eyes racing over the text as she read it aloud. 'Says Konrad Sulikov was born here. English mother, Polish father, moved there aged seven. Current whereabouts not known. Surveillance operation launched last year in connection with trafficking but we believe Sulikov was alerted to this and is in hiding. Photograph attached, jpeg file.'

Her fingers were trembling, her heart burning as she clicked the attachment. The customary warning came on: what would you like to do with this file? Janine selected open it. The loading bar appeared, a flash of blue as it processed the file and then the pixels filled the screen. A face. His face. Janine's eyes scurried over the features; she forced herself to slow down, look steadily and make sure: the long, bony nose, the slightly mismatched eyes, the chiselled cheekbone and dimpled jaw of James Harper. A few years younger, with a lower hairline, but unmistakeably the same man.

She heard exclamations from Richard's end, joined in with her own. 'Shit! The cheeky bugger. Konrad Sulikov otherwise known as James Harper.' And they'd released him! On bail, but it didn't take a rocket scientist to figure out he'd make a run for it.

'Airports!' she instructed Richard. 'Check the passenger manifests.'

'His house?'

'Send someone round, just to cover our backs, he won't be there. Get a technician too — I bet that's our scene. Come and get me.' She rang off. She kissed Tom's hair and told him to be good for Michael. She snapped shut the poppers on Charlotte's babygro, scooped her up and took her into the back room where Michael was enjoying a game on the Xbox. 'You have to watch her.'

'Mum!' He protested but he held his arms out anyway and Charlotte gave a little shriek of glee.

'I've got my phone,' she called as she pulled open the door, 'send Tom up in half an hour.'

Richard reached her in record time.

CHAPTER TWENTY-THREE

Shap had just treated himself to a cold Guinness when his phone went.

'He's not going to show,' Butchers told him.

'How come?'

'He's the invisible man.'

'If this is some sort of wind–up . . .'

'It isn't. We're on our way to his place now. Boss wants you there pronto.'

'Poland?' Shap grabbed his glass and necked the top third.

'Harper's.'

'You what?'

'Now.' Butchers cut him off.

Shap took to his feet and raced out of the building. Behind him the receptionist frowned in consternation. She was sure she hadn't missed Mr Sulikov.

* * *

'The date of birth he gave us,' Richard said as she climbed into the car, 'you were right. That James William Harper died aged five, back in 1967.'

'Stolen identity. So Harper was just a cover for Sulikov all along. When things got hairy in Poland he comes over here and lives as Harper for the duration.'

'They're checking the airports now. Promised me it wouldn't take long.'

At Harper's house the officers who gained entry found the place deserted. The luminal light the technician carried showed extensive blood traces on the garage floor.

Janine stabbed at her phone when it rang. 'Konrad Sulikov is listed on the last flight from Manchester to Berlin. Departing twenty-one ten,' the voice on the other end informed her.

Janine checked her watch. It was five to. Her heart sank; no way would they make it. Sulikov would be seated by now. They'd be waiting for clearance to take off. 'But there's a delay,' the voice continued, 'one of the earlier flights had to be grounded and it's had a knock-on effect.'

'Yes! How long?' Janine swore as Richard took a corner far too fast.

'They've only just called them for boarding.'

She turned to Richard: 'Terminal One.' He nodded and increased his speed, the blues and twos, lights and siren, signalling their urgency to the rest of the traffic on the motorway.

She dialled Butchers. 'Terminal One, Berlin flight. Shap with you?'

'Just got here.'

'Good. Alert Airport Police, he's travelling as Konrad Sulikov, but tell them I want to handle this one personally,' she ended the call.

Janine thought for a moment. 'Everyone dealt with Harper,' she began. 'Sulikov was there in the background, the big bogey man. Marta, the others, they knew of his reputation — you saw what they were like when his name came up, but it was all hearsay, whispers. Talked up by Harper. No one here ever met Sulikov. Hang on,' there was a flaw in the argument, 'Stone saw Sulikov shoot Gleason.'

'No, no,' Richard argued, 'he couldn't see! It was dark; they were ambushed. Stone saw Gleason fall and he scarpered. He expected it to be Sulikov because they'd spoken on the phone.'

'That's right.'

'Stone told me he occasionally got calls from Sulikov, fetch this, carry that. They had no need to meet and Stone assumed Sulikov was in Poland, like we did. Then he gets the call offering the pair of them easy passage across the Channel. Sulikov just happens to be in Manchester.'

'Very convenient.'

Richard increased his speed as they reached the motorway and moved into the outside lane.

'Harper's the good bloke,' Janine mused, 'fair bloke, looks out for the girls whereas Sulikov is the ruthless boss, whose reputation goes before him. Lots of gangsters use different names, half-a-dozen passports; but he took it much further. He created Harper as an alternative identity, an insurance policy. He might not need to use it but last year, when they started looking into his people trafficking in Poland, Sulikov goes to ground and Harper comes to life.'

'An exit strategy,' Richard said.

Janine laughed at the jargon. 'Presumably he can switch his accent on and off to suit the occasion, he's bi-lingual,' she said. 'So as Harper he killed Rosa at his place. She's about to run off, she's pregnant, wants out.'

'Maybe she threatens to blow the gaffe about everything, the brothel, the trafficking, the lot,' Richard suggested.

'Yes, I don't think he planned it, though. It was all too messy. If he'd wanted her removed, he'd have organised a contract killing or something that left him unsullied. It's more likely that they argued, Harper loses it, and flips. He strangles her. Then he has a body on his hands. He's got to hide his tracks. He messes her face up, removes the tattoo . . .' Janine's stomach turned at the thought of Harper hitting Rosa's face, desperately trying to obliterate her, '. . . parcels her up, weights and all. Then, as Sulikov, he rings Stone.'

Richard said, 'He lies about it, says she's OD'd. Harper drives the car to the industrial estate, leaves it for Stone. Then he goes home and reports his car stolen. He told Stone and Gleason to get rid of Rosa and torch the car. He expected that to be the end of it. No body; she's at the bottom of the Mersey, and no car; that's gone up in flames. Everything carries on as normal.' Richard glanced at her; she nodded. She picked up the thread.

'Might all have been hunky dory if the lads had got rid of the car straight away as Harper intended but the hit and run put paid to that.'

'When that happens Harper wants shot of Stone and Gleason, they know too much . . . and we're getting closer all the time. So he ambushes them and shoots Gleason.'

'But Stone gets away.'

'That's when he booked the hotel!' Janine shouted triumphantly. 'Wednesday night,' she hurried on, 'he needed to distract us — send us after Sulikov, make the guy look real.'

Richard tapped the brake as a four wheel drive slowed in front of them. The car jerked throwing them both forward.

'Christ!' Janine said.

'Sorry.' Richard watched the vehicle in front move over and then he roared forward.

'Naming Sulikov was the ace up his sleeve. We could have been sitting there still, like a load of wallies, waiting at the Midland for the man, while he's airside, studying the in-flight mag and having his complimentary G&T.' She turned to Richard, her face glowing with excitement. 'And the way he made us drag it out of him,' she hit the dashboard, 'can you credit it? In fear for his life.' She shook her head.

'Give the man an Oscar.'

'He's bloody good,' Janine said, 'but we're better.'

The car squealed to a halt outside the Departures Area. They raced in. They made their way through a mass of Mancunians, Scousers and Geordies returning from holidays in the sun. Dressed in thin cotton clothes, sporting red peeling noses or tans the colour of cheap wood dye, they pushed trolleys towering high with luggage and carrier bags of in-flight cigarettes. Children clung on or trailed wearily in their wake. A baby screamed relentlessly.

Heading for departures, Janine and Richard showed their badges and were waved through passport control. Glancing back she saw Shap and Butchers behind them. Gate 8 was one of the nearer boarding gates but even so a fair distance from the departure lounge. They ran along the travelators, only slowing as they came in sight of the boarding gate.

Harper was among other passengers huddled round the desk, boarding passes in hand. Janine could see him speaking rapidly into a mobile phone.

As they drew closer, she could hear he wasn't speaking English; she guessed it was Polish. No doubt making plans to disappear once he got to Germany. He wore a warm, camel overcoat, a smarter look than she'd come to expect from Harper. His hair was slicked back too. But it was his stance more than anything that had altered. Sulikov held himself upright, he'd the assurance of a professional, he appeared energetic in contrast to the slightly shabby, gutless persona of Harper.

'Mr Sulikov,' she kept her tone light. He turned. His face changed as he saw them, a flare of anger then resignation. 'Konrad Sulikov,' she smiled, 'I am arresting you on suspicion of the murders of Rosa Milicz and Jeremy Gleason. You do not have to say anything. But it may harm your defence if you do not mention something which you later rely on in court. Anything you do say may be given in evidence. Is there anything you would like to say?'

He simply stared at her, his mouth twisted in a spasm momentarily. Janine felt the pressure in her chest ease and relief edge down her spine. Got him. She nodded to Butchers who stepped forward with the cuffs.

* * *

Afterwards, as they made their way back through the airport along the travelators, Richard was teasing her. OK, she was swaggering a little. Why the hell not? It had been a killer of a case.

'You are such a show off!' he said.

'If you've got it . . . You didn't do so bad yourself, you know.'

'Need to seal off his place, see what else we can find. A telltale brick, perhaps.'

She grimaced. 'The blood and the DNA'll clinch it.'

'It'll keep till morning. He's got to have his eight hours, by rights.'

'More than I'll get.' Then thinking about Rosa, about the whole sorry story, 'Why couldn't he just let her go? None of this . . .'

'Crime of passion?'

'No, I don't think he cared for her. Marta was right. He killed her to protect himself. Back home with a baby, his baby, she'd be beyond his control. He did it in the heat of the moment; he was probably enraged but it was fear of what he might lose rather than anything else. Once he'd done it, he blamed Sulikov, and turned it to his advantage — look what might happen if you rock the boat. Except we found Rosa and it all started to unravel.'

'Do you think Rosa ever knew? About Sulikov?'

'How could she? He'd never have told her. She was just another girl. A way of making money.'

Rosa gone, Ann-Marie gone, Jeremy Gleason gone. There may well have been others, she thought, over the years, silenced by Sulikov if they threatened his empire. Bystanders too, hit by the violence inherent in his enterprises. There may well have been some truth in the myth of the ruthless criminal.

She remembered the little dictionary Rosa had studied; she hoped to teach, Marta had said. She thought of Debbie and Chris Chinley, adrift on the wreck of their lives. The loss of Ann-Marie would define them for ever. And Jeremy Gleason's mum, burying her wayward son; and a little boy who would grow up to find out one day that his dad had been walking on the wrong side of the tracks, had been shot and killed one miserable Manchester night.

'Good to have you back,' Richard said.

'You've changed your tune. You weren't saying that when Hackett passed you over.'

'No, really.' He looked intent. 'I'd forgotten.' He dipped his head towards her. 'You and me — something special.'

She felt a small swirl of panic, a thrill of nerves in her stomach as she recognised he was flirting with her. Just play the game, she told herself, enjoy it. He knows it's early days, what with the baby and everything. 'You reckon?' Her mouth felt dry.

'Oh, aye, always have done.'

She waited, wondering if he'd ask her out again, hoping he wouldn't, not wanting to disappoint him. But he left it at that. Smiled and shook his head at her.

She folded her arms and stared at the adverts installed along the walls, touting Manchester to the world, a place for culture, business and opportunity. In the arrivals hall they skirted the mêlée of baggage reclaim. The hall looked seedy, she thought, undermining the gloss of the advertising, harsh lighting, scuffed paint. In need of a makeover.

A wave of fatigue crashed over her. She could sense the downer waiting, the peculiar limbo that followed a catch. Still plenty to do but none of the adrenalin that kept them all going.

Richard stopped her at the door. 'Janine.'

Oh no, she thought. Not another declaration. Not now. She shook her head.

'You'd rather get a taxi?'

Damn! She gave him a sour grimace. 'No.'

'What did you think I was going to say?'

'Nothing.'

'Go on, what?' he insisted as they passed through the big glass doors.

'Nothing.'

'There was.'

'Richard, leave it.'

They got into his car, bickering gently. She settled back and let him drive her home through the cold, dark, rain drenched night.

THE END

ACKNOWLEDGEMENTS

Thanks to everyone involved with *Blue Murder* at Granada and specially to Anna Davies — a brilliant script editor.

ALSO BY CATH STAINCLIFFE

DETECTIVE JANINE LEWIS MYSTERIES
Book 1: BLUE MURDER
Book 2: HIT AND RUN

Thank you for reading this book.

If you enjoyed it please leave feedback on Amazon or Goodreads, and if there is anything we missed or you have a question about, then please get in touch. We appreciate you choosing our book.

Founded in 2014 in Shoreditch, London, we at Joffe Books pride ourselves on our history of innovative publishing. We were thrilled to be shortlisted for Independent Publisher of the Year at the British Book Awards.

www.joffebooks.com

We're very grateful to eagle-eyed readers who take the time to contact us. Please send any errors you find to corrections@joffebooks.com. We'll get them fixed ASAP.

Printed in Dunstable, United Kingdom

79955971R00109